# WANTING A WITCH

## A WINTER SOLSTICE ROMANCE

## LAUREN CONNOLLY

 Created with Vellum

*For the women who fall in love with witches.*

**1**

―――――

**KETA**

*Ring the doorbell, you coward.*

My words of motivation could do with a positive spin.

*Ring the doorbell, you powerful goddess of the night.*

I smile to myself and reevaluate the entrance to the townhouse. The front porch light is on, creating a warm pool in the chill of the early morning darkness.

Not that I'm particularly cold. Before getting out of my van, I shrugged on the puffy yellow coat I'd bought from a thrift shop last winter. But more importantly, I fed just a few days ago.

The donor's blood pulses through my veins with a subtle heat and a tingle of energy, which I pull on now to fuel my courage.

Wooden porch steps creak as I mount them, the sound overly loud in the quiet night. But their chorus is nothing compared to the echoing ring of the doorbell. The chime reverberates through the house, and I pray to the gods that the owner doesn't go straight to bed after her night shift.

Luckily, my supernatural hearing doesn't pick up any muttered cursing or threats. There's just the muffled shuffle of footsteps a moment before the lock turns and the door swings open.

Finally, after years of imagining, I get my first look—a good look, not clouded by pain or drugs—at Roe Fowler.

The woman who saved my life.

"Wow." The word sneaks out before I consider how strange of a greeting it is.

But my brain struggles to provide anything else.

Because Roe Fowler is *wow*.

Even wearing wrinkled scrubs that smell like anesthetic and sporting blocky rubber shoes that appear more durable than steel-toed boots, the woman is striking.

Her mostly angular face has lush lips, the bottom one dipping slightly in the middle. An indent perfect for running a tongue along. I lick my own lips at the fantasy and try to formulate a coherent thought.

The task is difficult to accomplish with her staring. Dark eyes beneath sharp brows examine me, slicing through my skin as if any barrier I try to erect between us would give as easily as tissue paper.

"Can I help you?" The rasp of her voice drags across my eardrums in an erotic caress.

*I want you.*

The intensity of that thought shocks me out of my lusty disconnect from reality.

I didn't come to Roanoke to ogle a sexy woman. I have two errands to complete in this city, and neither involves eye-fucking Roe Fowler.

"You already did help me," I say. "That's why I'm here actually."

Confusion crinkles the space between her brows, and I lose

my breath at how the expression reveals she's not only beautiful, but also adorable.

*What's next? Kind? Intelligent? Funny?*

This is not a good time to find myself in front of my fantasy
woman. I have things to do.

"Do I know you?" Her eyes, the same intriguing blackness
as the space between stars in a night sky, skim over me,
searching for something familiar.

I try not to let the lack of recognition dishearten me. I'm
nothing like I was the day our lives first intertwined.

"Not exactly. But we have met before. Kind of." For some
reason, I never considered exactly what I would say when I
came face-to-face with the woman who had rescued me.
"Remember the patient you had a few years ago who had been
drained by vampires? The one you called your friend Uma
about? Well ..." I step back and spread my arms, letting her
connect the rest of the dots.

As a nurse, Roe has probably had lots of strange cases show
up in her emergency room. Maybe I'm not the only victim of a
supernatural attack she's treated, but I know for sure that I'm
the only one who was so far gone that she felt the need to call
in Uma Latimer's assistance.

Vampires assaulted me. Then, one saved me.

If there had been any other rescue missions, Uma would
have told me.

Until now, Roe has kept one hand on her door, as if ready to
slam it shut if I were some kind of threat to her. An understand-
able worry when a stranger rings your doorbell at five in the
morning. But now, her grip loosens, and she moves forward,
gaze more intense than before.

I have every ounce of her attention, and the sensation is
intoxicating.

"Keta?"

The sound of my name from her mouth is more delicious than the blood of a woman drunk on pinot noir.

*Maybe she'll let me record her saying it on my phone. That wouldn't be a weird request, right?*

*Stay on topic,* I scold myself.

"Keta Latimer, at your service."

I hold out my hand for her to shake, and after a moment of hesitation, she does.

I wonder if the reluctance arises from surprise or because she wants to avoid touching me.

Her palm is warm and rough where it clasps mine, and I command my grip to loosen after an acceptable amount of handshaking time has passed.

"You took Uma's last name?" Roe asks with a note of something in her voice I can't interpret.

"She said I could. And after Uma brought me back to life, I figured she was basically my new mom." Plus, I wanted to get rid of all the things connecting me to my life before the attack.

New name, new me, new chance at life.

Life as a vampire.

"Uma always wanted a daughter," Roe murmurs.

"I..." Words fade from my mouth as I absorb what she just said.

After living with Uma for six years, I thought I knew most everything there was to know about the vampire. But I guess everyone has their secrets. "Is that why you called her that night?"

Roe crosses her arms and leans on her doorframe. "No. I called her because you were dying, and human medicine wasn't going to save you. Neither was my magic. Only a vampire could, and she's the only vampire I know."

When I was nineteen and didn't care about my life, something like luck or fate landed me in the emergency room where

Roe Fowler was working. A normal nurse would have had to watch me succumb to my wounds. But this nurse also happens to be a witch. Because of her knowledge of the supernatural world, I'm alive today.

Well, more like undead. But I don't feel the need to make the distinction.

"Everything you did for me, that's why I'm here." Stepping closer, I hold her eyes with mine, hoping she can see the depth of sincerity in my soul when I speak. "Thank you."

Roe blinks and then tears her stare from mine, glaring at the porch beneath my feet while running an agitated hand through her hair. "I did my job."

"No." I want to take her hand again, rub my thumb over the well-earned calluses. "You could have gone the easy route. Kept up your human ruse and let me die. But you risked everything by letting Uma turn me and then sneak me out. And now, I have so much more than I ever thought I would because of you. And I know this is years late—I'm behind on a lot of things—but I needed to tell you in person that you are amazing, and every day, I'm thankful for you."

Roe swallows, and I watch the muscles move in her throat. Goddess, that is not a good place for me to be staring. The fantasy of my fangs slowly sliding into her flushed skin has my gums aching. My fangs want to descend.

Maybe I should've written this all in a note, like Uma suggested. My vampire mother said that Roe didn't do well with gratitude, but I was insistent that I deliver my thanks in person. Besides, I had to come to Virginia anyway. This trip has two missions. One of thanks and one of forgiveness. The first is easier, which is why I started here.

But now, I don't want to leave.

Which means I probably should.

Roe still hasn't said anything, seeming content to just stare at a spot on the ground while I stumble through my awkward thanks.

"Yeah ... so ... that's it." I shove my hands in my pockets and step back. "Just came to tell you that."

"You're leaving?" she asks, as if we had made plans to hang out and I was suddenly canceling at the last minute.

"Yes? I mean, that's why I came. I was just waiting for you to get home from work, so I could talk to you, and then I thought I'd head out."

Roe stops avoiding my gaze, the confused wrinkle back between her brows. "Waiting for me?" That's when she tilts her head, peering over my shoulder. "In that?"

She points across the street, and I know what she's gesturing toward.

"Yep. I got here around midnight and just hung out. Then, you came home, and I tried to catch you before you went to bed."

Roe studies me. "You spied on my house all night in a creepy van?"

"Whoa. Pump the brakes." I plant my fists on my hips and scowl at the witch. "I was not spying. I was *waiting*. And my van is not creepy."

Her gaze flicks behind me and then back to my face, unconvinced. "Sure."

Indignation drowns out some of my infatuation. "It's not! Okay, maybe the outside isn't sunshine and rainbows." In fact, the paint job is a matte black with darkly tinted windows. "But inside, it's comfy and cozy and the opposite of creepy. There are throw pillows in the back, for goddess's sake." I spent months refurbishing my van into a home on wheels in preparation for a cross-country road trip, and not even a woman as devastatingly gorgeous as Roe Fowler is allowed to insult it.

The witch only blinks at me, and I let out a huff.

"Whatever. I didn't come here to get your approval on my

vehicle. I came to say thank you, and that's done. Have a nice life."

Just when I'm about to turn and stomp back to my perfectly lovely van, her low voice stops me with a question.

"Do you drink tea?"

**2**

———

**KETA**

ROE IS SOAKING WET, and I'm sipping on a cup of chamomile.

Unfortunately, I don't have a view of the wet witch because she's upstairs, showering off her night of work, while I sit like a good little vampire at her kitchen table.

I'm not sure why I agreed to come in for tea. I don't normally drink anything—other than B negative. Now, I'm going to have to use a bathroom in a few hours, which is something I don't usually have to worry about. All my supernatural body needs is a healthy dose of blood once a month, and I'm set on nutrients for a while.

But when Roe gave me an opening, a reason to stay in her presence for even a short moment longer, my offense at her comments about my van evaporated, and I followed her inside. She left me with a mug of steaming water and a handful of tea bags before going to shower and change.

"My van is *amazing*," I mutter to the empty chair across from me.

Okay, my affront didn't disappear completely.

Little does Roe know, I could have been way creepier. I successfully suppressed the urge to pull out my camera while I was waiting. The moonlight hit the roof of the witch's house in an interesting way, and I considered trying to capture a shot of the glowing shingles.

Taking pictures of her house in the middle of the night while sitting in my van would have pushed me from waiting to spying.

Luckily, the commonsense portion of my brain determined I didn't need to verbalize that argument.

I'm about done with my drink when footsteps sound on the stairs, and a second later, Roe joins me in the kitchen.

*Dear goddess of the night, did she get hotter?*

The nurse dispensed with her scrubs, now sporting a very professional-looking set of pajamas. The shirt has actual buttons. And a collar.

My nicest bedclothes are barley opaque enough to hide my nipples. Mainly, I sleep in threadbare castoffs that would get me arrested for public indecency if I went outside in them.

However, even with the nicely ironed bedtime attire, Roe's outfit change reveals an edgy tilt to her appearance. The woman has tattoos twining up from her wrists. The designs stretch so far, I can't see an end as they disappear under her sleeves.

"I like your arms." The idiotic words blurt from my soul.

At this moment, I doubt anyone would believe that I ever got paid to flirt with people.

I did. I was good at it.

But to be fair to myself, Roe Fowler was never one of my clients.

That I know of.

She leans back on the counter, crosses said arms over her chest, and raises a single eyebrow as she stares at me.

The pose is so sexy, I almost melt into a gooey puddle of lust at her feet.

Instead, I continue to run my mouth. "Your tattoos, I mean. I like the tattoos on your arms. Those are words, right? The language used by witches? I've seen it in spell books before. It's beautiful. I always thought the letters looked like plants. Like they grew on the page instead of someone having written them down."

*Shut up*, I scold myself.

Roe's lips tighten, but I can't tell if she's fighting a frown or a smile.

"There's a witch in Colorado," she says after a moment of silence. "Great with a tattoo gun."

*Of course.* I can imagine how the covens would be in an uproar if someone asked a human artist to write in the sacred script. Even if only witches can read the words. An innate ability all of their kind are born with.

There was a time that I longed to decipher the meaning of the letters more than I wanted anything else in the world. Many nights, I would bring on vicious migraines as I stared at the nonsensical lines for hours.

Despite never discovering the secrets of the language, I still find the mysterious text enchanting. More so when etched into the skin of a gorgeous woman.

"What do they mean?" I ask before realizing my mistake. My entire body tightens in defense, bracing for her rejection.

Instead, Roe stretches both her arms out, slowly rotating them so I can view every inch.

"Spells to draw power and store it. My family's magic is mainly fueled by suffering." She grimaces.

"The Fowlers get a bad reputation for that?" I guess. As a blood drinker, I can commiserate.

People don't like strangers feeding off them, especially when they're in pain.

Roe runs a palm along her forearm. "Some ancestors deserved it. The ones hungry for power caused suffering just to get more." She finger-combs damp strands of hair out of her eyes, and I catch a tart yet sweet scent in the air. "But I find plenty on the job."

A hospital has to be overflowing with people radiating physical and emotional pain.

"And you're a healer?"

"Yes."

"So, you're like a solar panel," I offer with a grin.

Roe tilts her head, gaze back on me.

"You draw energy from people because they're hurting and then use that to heal them," I explain. "You're a renewable resource!"

A sardonic smile tugs up the corners of her mouth. "You could say that."

For a time, the curves of her face mesmerize me. With my eyes, I trace the sweep of her brow, the angle of her chin, the dip in her bottom lip.

*I want her.*

"How's Uma?" she asks, pulling me out of my inappropriate staring.

Gathering my thoughts, I try to pretend I wasn't just fantasizing about the taste of her skin against my tongue.

"She's good. Teaching night classes. Her students love her." But then, everyone loves Uma. "Sad to see me go. I'm going to miss her."

The woman claimed the vacant place in my heart where a mother's love should go. But I couldn't live under her roof forever. There are things I need to do. Loose ends from my past I need to knot up, so I can move on and build a life.

"I miss her too," Roe murmurs, as if to herself, fiddling with her collar.

"She tutored you for college, right?"

"Yes. But she has been around my whole life. Like an aunt."

"You never visited her." The statement is out before I realize how accusatory it sounds. I want to take it back, especially when Roe drops her eyes to the checkered tiles beneath our feet.

"No. Not for a while."

*Why?* The question hangs in the air, but I don't ask, and she doesn't volunteer an answer.

Sure that I've neatly screwed up this gratitude trip, I clear my throat and glance toward the door. "Thank you for the tea, but I should probably let you get to bed."

"The sun is almost up." Roe jerks her chin toward the clock above the oven.

The witch is right. I've got maybe twenty minutes before that fiery orb crests the horizon and my life becomes a sunshine obstacle course.

"Shit," I mutter to myself, doing the math in my head. If I push my van over the speed limit, I might still make it. "I really have to go."

"You have a place to sleep for the day?"

"There's a campground right outside city limits." I stand up from my chair, only to get stopped by a hand on my arm.

"You're sleeping in a tent?" Concern colors her voice and pinches her brow.

The worry has me grinning. People caring about me is a newer experience, and I bask in the attention.

"Don't worry; I'm not in a tent. I sleep in my van. That thing is as dark as a moonless midnight when I shut it up."

She shakes her head. "That can't be safe."

"Did you forget who turned me? I'm a Daylighter, like Uma. The sun won't kill me even if it does get through somehow."

"It doesn't have to be deadly to be dangerous."

Roe has me there. Just because I can walk around at high

noon without burning to a crisp doesn't mean I don't have a reason to worry. Still, I shrug.

"I didn't budget for a hotel, so it's all I've got. And I need to get on the road. Like, now." But even as I take another step toward the door, Roe doesn't let go of my arm.

"Stay here." Her fingers tighten briefly and then release. "I have a spare bedroom. With blackout curtains."

Some precious traveling time is lost as I comprehend her statement.

*This witch is offering me a bed? In her home?*

*That ... can't be right.*

But then I recall her tone. Not spontaneous. Commanding.

"Did you do this on purpose?" I try to meet her eyes without sinking into their fathomless depths.

"Do what?"

"Keep me until the sun is about to rise. Until it's too late for me to go." Even though I speak the words with afront, I'm secretly harboring a glow of anticipation.

*Could the witch feel this attraction too?*

Roe moves away, grabbing my mug off the table and rinsing it in the sink. "You're not a prisoner. But I'd rather you stay in my spare room than your van."

*Can I stay in your room?* I'm tempted to ask.

"I'll give you the code to the garage. Come and go whenever you want."

I love my van, but I can't deny how much I like the idea of being around Roe Fowler for a little longer. "You don't have a roommate who will mind? A partner?"

"No." Before my hopes can soar too high at her response, she keeps going, "My girlfriend has her own place."

"Oh." The word drifts out on a low, dejected note, so I immediately cover it up with fake enthusiasm. "Okay! I'll stay with you. I have some business in Roanoke, but it shouldn't take long." Just the time required for me to gather my courage. "I'll be gone in a day or so."

"That's fine." She dries off the mug and places it in the cabinet. "Let me show you the room."

As I follow the witch upstairs, watching the way her slim hips sway with each step, I wonder if I've just signed myself up for a torturous experience.

No firm answer on that yet, but there is one thing I know for sure.

I'm going to need to buy some new pajamas.

**3**

———

**ROE**

**Three Weeks Later**

SOMETIMES, I wonder if Keta intends to torture me.

I can imagine her waking up in the evening and asking herself, *What new way can I drive Roe mad with lust?*

Tonight, she's settled on a pair of sleep shorts that tease me with the bottom curves of her ass cheeks. And she's not simply standing in them. Instead, my temporary vampire roommate dances around while using a spatula as a prop microphone in her impromptu routine.

The pink headphones covering her ears keep me from hearing the music. When I pause at the kitchen table, I spot her phone. With a single finger, I turn the device toward me and read the screen. Not a big surprise that she's listening to a Top 40 station. Keta is a pop-music kind of woman. Always searching out a beat that gives her a chance to swing her hips.

I've found the hits more appealing ever since she's started staying with me.

Keta Latimer has cast a different light on many things since moving into my house.

For one, I discovered that my kitchen has more functions than just a room for my microwave.

*Who would've thought a being that can't eat would cook so much?*

For the past few weeks, I've come downstairs, ready to leave for work, only to find a breakfast waiting for me. Like I'm wealthy enough for a live-in chef.

I've tried not to get used to the kindness, not wanting to add another loss to the day Keta eventually leaves. And since I'm not working my normal shift today, I thought I'd be fending for myself.

A quick glance at the clock tells me sunrise is only an hour away. My roommate should be getting ready for bed, not shimmying in front of the stove.

"Keta."

She doesn't respond, just keeps swaying her body, threatening to hypnotize me.

"Keta," I say louder but still no sign she heard.

With a sigh, I cross the kitchen, traversing the space I was trying to keep between us, and give her a gentle poke in the ribs.

The vampire screeches, whirling with supernatural speed and chucking something against my chest. There's a soft *thwap* and then the clatter of metal hitting the floor. Glancing down, I find my previously clean scrubs are now dripping with batter.

"Goddess! You scared me!" Keta pushes her headphones off, observing me with wild eyes. Her blond curls bounce as she springs into action, grabbing a handful of paper towels off the roll. "I'm sorry. You're a mess."

She tries to scoop the batter off my clothes, wiping the front of my shirt with firm strokes. When her touch passes over my chest, my nipples tighten, pressing against the cotton of my sports bra. It's all I can do not to gasp. Or moan.

Instead, I step away, heading for the stairs. "I'll change. Don't throw anything else at me when I come back down."

"I'm sorry!" Her repeated apology follows me all the way to my bedroom.

Sparing a quick, longing glance at my sheets, I imagine for a moment that I have time to crawl under them and touch myself to the memory of what just occurred in my kitchen.

With a frustrated sigh, I throw my soiled top into the hamper and grab a clean one from my dresser.

Back downstairs, I find Keta sitting at my kitchen table, wearing a contrite expression as she clutches a cup of orange juice. Across from her, on the place setting where I normally sit, is a stack of what looks to be blueberry pancakes with a side of bacon.

My stomach growls in appreciation.

"You didn't have to do this," I say, even as I settle in front of the feast.

Keta shrugs. "It's fun to cook for you."

"It's late for you to be up."

My roommate takes a sip of her juice, not bothering to respond.

The vampire stayed up to cook for me. She's never needed to make me any meal, but she still does.

As I cut into the pancakes, their sugary aroma surrounds me, and I have to close my eyes when the first bite touches my tongue. Despite Keta's lack of appetite, she knows how to create some mesmerizing flavors.

When I blink, I find her gaze on me, so focused that I wonder if she'd hear the fire alarm go off.

"You're watching me eat again," I point out, my voice as dry as I can manage when my entire body is on fire for her. This seems to be a habit of hers. I wonder if she misses food.

"Sorry. Does that make you uncomfortable?"

"No."

*Yes.*

But not in the way she means. It makes me uncomfortably hot. Makes me uncomfortable in my king-size bed because I suddenly want someone beside me in it.

"If you invite your girlfriend over, I could stare at someone else while they ate," she throws the comment at me across the table.

"She's not interested in coming over." My attention stays on the piece of crispy bacon I'm breaking in half, just to give my hands something to do.

"Because of me?" Keta sounds legitimately concerned. Like the thought of me fucking another woman just a door down from her doesn't bother her.

"No."

Candace isn't interested in coming over because I broke things off with her three weeks ago. The night after Keta first crashed at my place.

Two completely unrelated events.

Besides, I only thought the vampire was staying for a couple of days.

Somehow, that's expanded to close to a month.

And for someone who values their alone time, I'm constantly surprised at how I don't mind my new roommate. Keta keeps a similar night-owl schedule to me, only listens to music with her headphones on, cleans up after herself, and has gotten in the habit of cooking me a different culinary creation every day.

She's made waffles, French toast, omelets, eggs in every possible variation, paired with all the different breakfast meats. There's never been a time in my life when I was more well-fed.

Keta is the perfect person to live with.

In fact, she seems very close to the perfect woman. Someone who should have something better to do than feed a taciturn witch.

I can't figure her out, and every night, my curiosity only grows.

Now, I'm the one staring across the table.

Keta doesn't look like a traditional vampire. No pale complexion or willowy figure. She's strong and curvy with goldenly tan skin. Her hair rings her face, further softening already-round cheeks. Keta Latimer gives every appearance of a summer child, best suited for wearing a pair of roller skates and cruising down a boardwalk in California.

So different from the first time I saw her.

The memory hits me hard, curdling the food in my stomach.

Keta was pale that night. Drained of blood and on the edge of death.

*"Two bite marks on the sides of the neck. Three bite marks on the upper right arm. Laceration approximately four inches long on the left wrist. Two bite marks on the upper left arm. Five bite marks on the upper right thigh. Two bite marks on the upper left thigh. All bites are of an unknown origin."*

The doctor's voice rolls through my mind, clear despite the years that have passed since I heard the list of injuries.

In that moment, as I worked in tandem with two other nurses to carefully rotate the patient's body for the doctor's examination, the truth registered.

*Vampire attack.*

With that realization, I burned with frustration. I knew that it wouldn't matter how many IVs we inserted in the woman's veins. Even with a rapid transfusion of type O, even if we could replace every single drop she'd lost, there was nothing mortal doctors could do to save her.

Because of how she had been bled.

Vampires, the kind Keta had run into, had fed off more than just blood. If they wanted, they could tap directly into their prey's life force. When that essential part of a being was sapped, only supernatural intervention could hope to heal the wound.

Even my abilities could only do so much. I pulled on the magic stored in the ink on my arms, the sensation like hundreds of hooks tugging on the skin. I encouraged the sluggish beating of her heart and discovered a small drop of vampire blood that had seeped into her veins.

One of her attackers had been sloppy.

Thank the goddess. That small amount, directed by my powers, was enough to keep Keta from succumbing to death. But only just.

After relocating the patient to the ICU, I stole a moment to call the one vampire I knew. The only being capable of saving the stranger who I'd latched on to in a way a nurse never should. Luckily, Uma picked up and broke all kinds of traffic laws to drive from Ohio to Virginia in time to save my patient.

She saved Keta.

*You almost died.* The horrified thought weaves through my head as I stare across the table at a woman so vibrant, it seems criminal to consider a world where she doesn't exist.

With a second chance at life, Keta should be out, chasing her dreams. Instead, she's loitering in a witch's townhouse at the end of a frosty Virginia autumn.

Keta catches my eye then, grinning eagerly under the attention.

"Still hungry? There's a couple more."

Before I can voice an opinion, the vampire is out of her chair and back at the skillet.

I'm pondering if my stomach can handle any more food when a familiar caw has Keta shrieking and chucking the spatula, pancake and all, at the kitchen window.

"Goddess-damn it!" She clutches her chest and glares through the glass at the crow perched on the sill. "You and that bird are trying to give me a heart attack!"

Noir lifts her wings in an avian shrug and then gives a light yet demanding tap with her beak on the glass.

"Maybe you should stop throwing items when you're scared." I fight a smile.

Keta glares over her shoulder at me, even as she unlatches the window for my familiar. The crow usually shows up whenever she feels like it, and as dramatic as Keta is, the vampire knows how much Noir means to me. She would never *intentionally* bludgeon my companion with a breakfast pastry.

A cold breeze accompanies the crow as it glides inside, alighting on a sturdy perch I built for her beside the table.

"Maybe you should populate your house with more pillows, so my projectiles aren't as harmful." Even though she sounds put out, Keta still pours a handful of peanuts into her cupped palm and offers the food to my familiar. Noir carefully plucks at the pieces, never piercing the vampire with her sharp beak.

No matter how hard I fight against the urge, I watch the pair with an ache in my chest. Something like longing.

The day I invited Keta to stay with me, I thought my attraction to her was fleeting, easily ignored. It's not like anything could happen between the two of us. For one, she's leaving town. Eventually.

But more than that, I have Uma's words in the back of my mind. The vague information my friend gave me six years ago when I called to check in on the mystery patient.

*"She made it through. I've got a newborn vampire living with me now."*

*"That must be fun."*

*Through the phone, I could hear joy in Uma's voice. "It is. She's …*

*well, she's kind of amazing. Sweet and funny. It's been years since I laughed this much. Thank you for calling me. The world would've lost a light if she'd passed on."*

*"Good to hear. I'll have to visit, so I can meet her properly."*

*When Uma didn't immediately respond with enthusiasm, I knew something was wrong.*

*"I'm not sure that's the best thing for her," my friend murmured.*

*"Why not?"*

*"I don't want to break her confidence, but what I can tell you is that she's no stranger to witches. And the ones she's dealt with hurt her. Now, I'm not saying you would. But she's going to be in a delicate state for a while. It might be better if she didn't have contact with any witches for the foreseeable future."*

At the time, I was disappointed but not overly hurt. The woman Uma described sounded like someone I'd want to meet but not if me being around her would be uncomfortable.

So, I put a pause on my visits to Uma and tried to forget about the new vampire.

But now, I can't seem to think of anything but Keta. Which is making it hard to encourage her to move along in her journey.

Keta was supposed to be done with her business in Roanoke weeks ago. And yet, she's still here, in my house, driving me mad with longing because she's everything Uma described and more.

But a woman hurt by witches isn't going to want to be with a witch even if she's willing to accept her hospitality.

As I get up from the table to put my dishes in the washer, the question hangs in the air. The one I'm supposed to ask.

*When are you heading out?*

But I never ask it. I'm too afraid of the answer. Terrified that

Keta will point to a pile of packed bags I didn't notice and claim she'll be on the road minutes after the next sunset.

Despite their brief tiff, Keta is now feeding my animal companion a second handful of peanuts and cooing to the creature as if Noir were a sweet little songbird.

"I'm going." I tip my head toward the front door. There wasn't any need for me to announce that. It's not like we're a couple, involved in each other's days.

*Just walk out the door*, I tell myself.

Instead, my body holds still until Keta acknowledges me again.

"Okay!" She wipes her hands off on those ridiculously short pajamas. "Bedtime for me."

The vampire moves to pass me, toes pointed toward the staircase. But she pauses at my side, leaning close to press her lips against my cheek in a fleeting move.

"Have a good day!"

Then, she's gone.

Alone, I raise my fingers to caress the spot, as if applying pressure will make the sensation permanent.

*What was that? Why did she do that?*

It takes everything in me to grab my bag and head out to the car, like there's nothing out of the ordinary. When I'm in the front seat, I unleash my sexually frustrated groan.

Keta is an affectionate woman. I bet she didn't even realize what she was doing. Or if she did, it was a silly joke to her.

If only I could convince my heart to be as uncaring.


**KETA**

*I kissed Roe.*

Damn the gods. She just smelled so good. Like raspberries and blood.

"I need to feed," I mutter as I toss in my bed again.

Normally, I can fall asleep easily in Roe's guest bedroom. I've been doing it for weeks now, somehow stifling the guilt of long overstaying my welcome. But today, I have a hint of her on my mouth. For the thousandth time, I run my tongue over my lips, like I'll somehow find a stray drop of her blood there.

*Why am I torturing myself like this?*

Roe is dating someone. Besides, she's a witch. Maybe she doesn't despise vampires like the others of her kind do, but I doubt she's interested in sleeping with one.

Meanwhile, I'm just lurking in her house, fostering this massive, unrequited crush.

It's childish.

Doesn't matter how many meals I make for her. She doesn't have to say it for me to know I'm an unwelcome guest.

And now, I'm a hungry one too.

My insides are both tight and hollow. The orange juice I drank this morning has done nothing for this body of mine.

There's only two ways I can get the nutrients I need. The first—and most obvious—is to find a willing vein to tap. Blood would immediately replenish everything I'm missing. Just the thought of that warm liquid filling my belly has my fangs aching.

But this need for blood reveals just how unprepared I was to leave Ohio.

Uma had an established set of close friends who knew what we both were and happily offered to act as donors once a month.

In Roanoke, I don't know anyone.

Not anyone who can help with this anyway.

There are the people from my childhood, but none of them are a feeding option.

If I'd known I would be staying this long, I would've been more social. There's a nice cashier who works the late shift at the grocery store. We chatted for a while about her grandkids, and she enjoyed hearing about my photography work.

Still, not really the foundation for asking to bite her neck.

I guess I should count myself lucky that I only have to do this once a month. There are other vampires who need to feed daily. Of course, they have skills to make the endeavor easier. All I have is my natural charisma.

As searching for a blood source becomes less appealing, the more I think about it, my mind drifts toward the other avenue I have for filling the cells of my body with all the nutrients they're starved for. Arguably an easier method, although last time I tried it, Uma had to bail me out of jail.

That's a call I'd prefer not to make again.

The thought of having to phone Roe and tell her I'm behind bars and need something else from her is too humiliating to even contemplate.

*For goddess's sake, she already saved my life. Now, I'm just taking advantage, trying to excuse my clingy behavior as an extra-long way of repaying that favor.*

Shoving my face into a pillow, I groan in frustration.

After this morning's kiss, I know I can't put feeding off any longer. If I get too hungry, daily life will become dangerous.

I could bite Roe—or a stranger—in a fit of starvation.

No one wants that.

*Option two it is.*

I'll just have to take precautions to combat any mishaps.

**4**

———————

**ROE**

THE SUN SHINING BRIGHTLY as I arrive home from work throws me off-balance. With the short days approaching the solstice, I'm used to waking in the dark and returning in the dark. The only reason I'm not today is because I offered to cover a partial shift for another nurse.

One last day of work before my holiday.

I enter the townhouse as quietly as I can, assuming that Keta is still fast asleep upstairs.

Thoughts of my roommate bring to mind the affectionate good-bye she gave me this morning. The sensation of her lips against my skin haunted me for my entire shift. But even with my distracted mind, it was the best day on the job I've had in a while. Getting that send-off filled a lonely hole I hadn't realized was festering deep in my chest.

My body, my heart, wants to add her loving gesture to my routine. More nourishing than a daily vitamin.

But I'm kidding myself. The kiss meant nothing special to Keta.

After hanging my keys on the hook by the door, I wander into the kitchen for a snack, stumbling to a stop when I spot movement out the back window.

*That can't be what I think it is.*

Approaching the glass with caution, I lean over the sink until I can see my entire backyard.

Keta is standing in the middle of the grass with her face turned up toward the afternoon sky.

Barefoot.

Topless.

She sways in a dreamy, languid manner, different from the way she was dancing this morning. Now, she moves like a person high on something.

And I know exactly what the drug is.

The sun.

"Shit," I mutter, running my eyes over her exposed skin, pulling on my clinical detachment to ignore this intimate view of her body.

Keta flushes the deep red of a ripe tomato in every spot the sunlight touches. Luckily, she still has on a pair of yoga pants.

*Who knows how long that'll last?*

The more of her body exposed, the worse her recovery will be. The blissed-out expression on her face is going to disappear fast when the sun goes down.

Lucky for her, she has a healing witch for a roommate.

Pulling my phone from my pocket, I dial a familiar number.

"Hello?"

"Mom," I say by way of greeting.

"Roe Roe, it's good to hear from you. Calling about the solstice's logistics? Just stay over here, and we'll all drive to the gathering together."

"No. I mean, yes, that sounds fine. But that's not why I called." There's a magnetic notepad on the fridge, and I grab it along with a pen. "I need you to walk me through a spell."

"Really? Which one?" The heavy thunk of items shifting tells me she's rifling through her grimoires.

Many witches lock away their magical texts to keep them safe. My mother, on the other hand, likes to arrange the powerful books on a shelf in her kitchen. She says they're spelled against fire and theft, so why not put them in a place that's easy to grab?

"Something to treat a bad sunburn. I've a friend who sat out too long."

"Ouch. That's no fun. Give me a moment, and I'll find what you need."

"Thanks."

Through my own kitchen window, I continue to watch Keta as she starts to twirl, around and around like an item lost in space with no gravity to slow it down.

And goddess, with her constant rotations, it's impossible not to admire every inch of the vampire. An unprompted fantasy arises, where I get to explore her curves with my hands. With my tongue.

"Found it!" My mother's voice spears through my lust, and I swallow to clear the dryness from my mouth.

"Tell me."

After writing down the ingredients needed and the words to speak, I head upstairs and run a bath. Keeping the water at a lukewarm temperature, I dump in the herbs my mother listed off for me. I might not bother with cooking much, but I make sure to always have a well-stocked herb supply. Couldn't call myself a decent witch without one.

When everything is set to go, I firm up my professional shield and then step out my back door.

Keta has finished twirling, but she continues to sway to a rhythm no one else can hear. I'm glad I installed a privacy fence around my yard. The idea of anyone else seeing my vampire dancing half-naked brings out a wave of protective aggressiveness.

"Keta."

At the sound of her name, she turns to face me, her dreamy smile widening further.

"Roe! *Row, row, row your boat—*" She breaks off in a fit of giggles, the cheerful sound shivering through my body.

No human would look at Keta in this moment and think she's a vampire. A fairy maybe with the way her golden hair absorbs the sunlight as the strands lay against her bare breasts.

Goddess, the sight of her nipples, a ruddy strawberry pink, does things to me.

The rest of her skin has taken on a brilliant red hue, which does not bode well.

"Come inside. I've drawn you a bath," I coax.

"A bath?" Keta laughs again, the sound unrestrained and airy, like the clouds floating far above us. "I don't need a bath! I'm not dirty. In fact"—she does a cartwheel, landing properly, only to wobble when she stands straight—"I'm perfect!"

"You're sun drunk." I step closer and widen my arms, brainstorming how to herd her into the house without copping the feel my hands are begging for.

"You're sun sober," she mocks, eyes pointed in my direction but so unfocused that I'm not sure she actually sees me.

"If you mean, I haven't been day drinking, then that is correct." Taking another step forward, I try to make my voice more enticing. "Let's go inside together."

"Together?" That word captures her attention, and she bounces on her toes. "Are you taking a bath too?"

"I'm going to help you bathe." *And try my best to remain as unaffected as when I give a patient a sponge bath.*

Keta gasps and then grins with a mischievous tilt to her mouth. "I like that idea. Race you!"

The vampire sprints around me, faster than I could ever

hope to move. Worried what trouble she'll get into if I'm not by her side, I jog after her. By the doorway, I spot her discarded T-shirt, and I scoop it up on my way.

When I reach the bathroom, Keta is waiting by the edge of the tub. The water has a murky white quality to it.

"Did you fill this with milk?" she asks.

"No. There're herbs. To help soothe your skin."

Keta grins at me over her shoulder. "You take such good care of me."

Then, her fingers hook in the waistband of her pants, and I don't have the time or the urge to turn my head as she drags the fabric down her toned legs.

Pressing my knuckles against my lips, I barely stifle a groan. Her generous ass taunts and tempts me in equal measure.

Thankfully, she doesn't linger, immediately stepping into the tub, her naked body sinking below the opaque surface.

"Mmm. This feels good." Keta settles low in the tub, pointing a toe so it crests the surface and then disappearing the digit just as quickly. She chuckles at the small splashes she made.

If this were a normal bath, I'd leave her to her own devices, escaping the room in self-preservation. But the concoction I brewed is moot without my magic. Keta needs me to stay.

As I approach the tub, I run my fingers over my arms, pulling on the power leftover from my earlier shift. Most witches need more than just words and herbs to work a spell. They require a source of power.

If the winter solstice were happening tonight, there would be magic thick in the surrounding air, just waiting for a practiced hand to manipulate and redirect the energy. But that natural fuel is still two days away, which means I'm left with my normal method of leeching off a hospital waiting room full of miserable people.

Sometimes, I wish I could tell those strangers what I'm able to do. That way, I could apologize for using them but also share how their devastation at the loss of a loved one might mean I could bring a little girl out of a coma or keep an assault victim from bleeding out.

My magic isn't limitless. I cannot save everyone or heal every illness.

But sometimes, I'm the only thing tethering a person to the world of the living, clutching their life force tight as the human doctors patch up their body.

Luckily, Keta is not fighting for her life. This shouldn't be too draining of a task.

A familiar sensation skitters over my skin, as if hundreds of tiny hooks, attached to hundreds of tiny strings, were giving the gentlest tug of my flesh.

When I reach Keta's side, I drop to my knees and dip my hands in the water, muttering the words to the spell under my breath.

"What are you saying?"

*Shit.*

I didn't want to reveal that I'd be working magic on her. With Uma's vague warning regarding Keta and witches, I have no idea if the vampire will go into hysterics or a rage when she finds out that this is more than just water, bath salts, and pleasant-smelling herbs. Hopefully, the sunlight she got drunk off of will keep her mellow.

"A spell to heal your skin." I brace myself for her reaction, but she only sighs.

"Witch's language. Never learned how to speak that." Keta's tone is mournful, as if the skill was an opportunity that passed her by.

But of course, she didn't. Witch's language is not something to be learned. Only those of our kind can comprehend it, and they do so without study.

Utilizing the words to direct magic is a whole different matter. *That* takes practice.

"You don't mind?" My request for consent is coming late, but I realize now that I should've asked first. I'm too used to working my power over people who don't believe it exists. But Keta knows, so she should decide.

"Nope. Don't mind one bit." She cups some water and watches as it trickles through her fingers. "I like your voice. When you talk, I get all shivery."

My body locks in place, frozen by the intimate comment.

*Does my voice really affect her body? Could that mean she isn't turned off by what I am?*

More likely, she's just saying random things because she's drunk.

I work hard to convince myself of that because that belief is the only way I can continue this healing process with any sense of professionalism.

"People like my voice too," she declares with a frankness that indicates the vampire is stating a fact, not fishing for compliments.

I make an inarticulate noise in response, afraid I'll expose how easily she could seduce me with a few words.

"Do you know how I paid for college?" Keta sounds dreamy as she leans her head back on the edge of the tub. Every part of her relaxed.

Honestly, I never thought about it. My mother started a college fund for me the moment a seer told her she'd have a baby. Guess I took that support for granted.

"Did Uma help you?"

"No." The vampire rolls her head back and forth in a floppy shake. "She offered, but I said thank you, but no, thank you. She helped me find a job though. One that paid well. *Really* well."

"What was the job?" I'm praying the conversation will soon

distract me from the way the top curves of her breasts crest above the milky bath.

There's a quiver in my fingers that agitates the water as I continue to direct my magic into the healing mixture.

"Hello," Keta says. Only she doesn't speak like her normally chipper self or even the half-wasted version I just dragged in from outside. Instead, her voice is low with a husky twinge and a whole load of secrets hiding underneath it. "I'm glad you called. I've been so lonely here, in my bed, with no one beside me. Do you want to keep me company?"

If I thought Keta was tempting before, it's nothing when compared to the raging need she just stoked in me.

"What are you doing?" In an attempt to suppress my desire, my question comes out with a sharp edge.

"Oh, I don't do it anymore." The vampire chuckles, her eyes on the ceiling, as if watching a scene only she can view. "But I used to. Six nights a week."

"What—"

"Phone sex. The simplest way to say it. But I always thought of it as phone companionship."

"You got paid to have phone sex with strangers?"

The thought has a jealous longing irritating my nerves.

*How many other people got to hear Keta speak dirty words to them?*

*And why couldn't I have had that phone number?*

"Like I said, that's the simplified version." She lifts her arm from the water, gaze focused on the murky ripples her movement caused.

Needing to do something, I cup a handful of the healing mixture and pour the contents over her still-ruby-colored shoulders. As the droplets caress her skin, the irritation caused by the sun starts to fade.

Good thing she's a Daylighter.

There are three strains of vampirism: daylight, evening, and midnight. The evening vamps used to refer to themselves as Twilighters, but a certain series of books put a sparkly twist on that terminology, and they rebranded themselves.

Neither evening nor midnight vampires can deal with direct sunlight. Daylighters can, but if they stay out too long, their skin blisters like a human with sun poisoning. And Daylighters always stay out too long because of the manic effect the natural light has on them.

"I was good at that job."

*Hell, she's still talking about phone sex?*

I wish she'd tell me more about her current occupation. Whenever Keta details her latest photojournalism project for me over breakfast, I find myself enthralled.

Same is going to be true of this subject but in a much more torturous way.

"Want to know why I was so good?" She blinks up at me now as I pour more water over her shoulders. Her expression is so open, honest, that I know shutting her down would wound her.

*What kind of nurse would I be to hurt someone who's already vulnerable?*

"Why?"

Keta smiles and flicks water at me, the droplets forming black speckles on the front of my scrubs. "Because I know exactly what it's like to be lonely."

Just like that, my lust dims, and my heart breaks.

Keta has the air of an open book, always laughing and energetic and sharing funny anecdotes from her days. But I know nothing about her from before the moment she showed up in my ER. Not even how she'd stumbled into a nest of homicidal vampires.

"They were lucky to get to speak to you," I mutter.

"Aww, Roe. You're so sweet." She reaches up and boops my nose, her grin on the verge of wild. "Don't get me wrong. A few of them went dark and wanted me to say some pretty nasty things. But mainly, they just wanted to talk to someone real. To make a connection. So, I did that. Threw in a little dirty talk, of course. That's the job. But in the end, they felt less lonely."

The drunken tinge to her words is fading away as she talks, and a glance out the window shows me the sun is sinking behind the trees.

Keta falls quiet, even as she pushes the water around her to make small waves in the foggy liquid.

Concentrating on the final bit of power in my tattoos, I give the potion she's soaking in a last dose and then rest back on my heels and suck in a couple of deep breaths to stave off the light-headedness often following a drain of my magic.

The moment the sun fully sets, Keta's body language changes. The vampire stops her playful movements, her entire being going statue still. Then, as if needing to protect herself, she pulls her knees into her chest and wraps her arms around her legs. A tight ball of defensiveness.

"Can I have a moment?" she whispers.

"Sure." Even as I push to my feet, I find myself reluctant to leave the bathroom.

*What will pass between us the next time she meets my eyes?*

*Will this drive her to a final good-bye?*

"You can stay as long as you'd like," I offer without thought. "You don't have to be lonely."

Keta's only response is a jerky nod.

And so, I leave her on her own.


**KETA**

Embarrassment burns my skin hotter than if Roe had just left me to deal with the effects of the sun.

*I danced half-naked in front of her.*

*I told her about the phone-sex job.*

*I made her take care of me, even after she worked all day.*

The last one of those might seem like a choice on Roe's part, but after living with the woman for close to a month, I know one thing for sure. There's no way the nurse would leave someone to fend for themselves when they needed medical care. I forced her hand because I'd gotten wasted on sunshine.

The smart choice would've been to call Uma and find out if she knew anyone in Roanoke willing to let me feed from them. Instead, I acted the fool by drawing my nutrients from pure sunlight.

The ability to survive the day might seem like a gift for a vampire, but it's hard to appreciate the freedom when exposure sends me on something very much like an acid trip.

The robe I wrap around myself presses softly against my newly healed skin. Kneeling beside the tub, I breathe in a deep breath above the fragrant bath, picking up notes of chamomile and thyme.

Roe put this together for me. She spoke the witches' language and poured her magic into this water for me.

All while I babbled on like an idiot. If the witch didn't think I was ditzy before, she sure does now.

*"You can stay as long as you'd like. You don't have to be lonely."*

Mortification burns my throat.

Goddess, she must see me as beyond pitiful.

"This is it. I've been here too long. Time to go." When I say the words out loud, they hurt. But I know they're right.

First, I'll apologize to Roe for making her work, even when she's supposed to be off the clock. Then, I'll pack my bags and finally complete the other task I came to Roanoke for.

No more making excuses. I won't be a coward.

The robe is a thick terry cloth, and I pull the covering tighter, shielded by its warmth. When I exit the bathroom, I hear sounds of movement downstairs and head in that direction.

I must have been moping in the bathroom longer than I realized. Roe's hair is slicked back from her face, wet from a recent shower. She has on her preferred pajamas—a matching set with shorts and a button-up shirt.

She always looks rather dapper in the getup. My eyes trace the buttons, and my fingers twitch to slide them free of their holes.

*Stop it*, I chide myself, plunging my fists into the deep robe pockets, hoping that'll keep them from misbehaving.

"I'm sorry."

"For what?" Roe doesn't look at me as she arranges a teapot on the stovetop.

*Is she really going to make me replay the last hour?*

Still, I should probably clarify. She might think I'm only apologizing for sharing some intimate details from my past.

I'm not ashamed of my time working as a phone sex operator. In fact, I can thank my mild success in my current career to that job. When I was in my last year of my degree, graduation hinged on a capstone project. Taking a chance, I reached out to the fifty other women who worked for the call company. Only five responded, and of those, three agreed to be photographed.

The low number didn't surprise me. Many of my coworkers at the time were married, had families, and even had other day jobs. All that would have been at risk if they participated.

But the three, plus me, still made for a fantastic story. There was Alexia with her girlishly high voice, who liked to suck on lollipops while she worked because they made her feel sexy. There was Tatiana, who always wore a suit when taking calls because that was her profession and she treated it like one. Scarlett was the most fun to interview. The aspiring voice actress used the job as an opportunity to practice different accents and characters.

When a popular women's magazine immediately accepted

my story for publication, I knew I'd finally found what I was good at.

Telling stories with images and words.

So, *that's* not why I'm sorry.

But I never told anyone my talent for the job came from my own crushing loneliness.

Then, there's everything else Roe dealt with in pursuit of taking care of me.

She didn't deserve a minute of the hassle.

"You don't have to pretend like you didn't come home to a raging idiot vampire. Thank you for taking care of me. Again. I'm sorry I put you in that position."

This amazing woman saved my life, and I keep acting like a leech on hers.

*What is wrong with me? Did my childhood really break my brain this much?*

"Why did you go out in the sun?"

My urge is to just reiterate my apology and flee the room, but Roe deserves answers to any questions she has.

"I was hungry. Last I fed was before I came to town, and I don't know anyone here well enough to ask. Stupidly, I thought if I went outside just before sunset, I'd be able to handle myself. Guess I know better now."

Roe turns her back to the stove, gripping the edge of it so her elbows bend out to the sides like wings. Sometimes, it's so clear to me why Noir is Roe's familiar. They resemble each other, although I would say the witch is more elegant than the animal. The crow is a wobbly, flapping mess when it lands and takes off. Roe has a strong grace about her, closer to a hawk.

I can't help focusing on the shape of her body and arms. For one, they call to me. But also, the subject gives me an excuse to ignore how she won't meet my eyes.

"You know me." The statement is so quiet, I'm not sure I would have heard it without my advance senses.

*I know her? Does that mean ...*

*No. Impossible.*

I grew up with witches. With their words always in the back of my mind.

*"Vampires are leeches. Bloodsucking nuisances. To let one feed off you is the lowest form of insult. No proper witch would associate with their kind, much less offer a vein to one."*

Roe must have meant something else. Maybe she knows someone in town who doesn't mind being a feeder.

*That must be it.*

"You don't have to worry about finding me a blood source. I know I've overstayed my welcome. Goddess knows why you've put up with me for so long." My chuckle sounds forced to my own ears.

"You don't have to leave." The witch turns to fiddle with the teapot.

And suddenly, I'm frustrated. With her.

"Come on! I've been a pushy mooch! I shoved my way into your home and have been squatting here like a vagrant. Get tough with me! Kick me out!" I need her to tell me to leave, or I'm afraid I'll make up some excuse to stay, and then my days of tortured longing will only continue.

Roe seems to ignore me at first, moving around, reaching for things on the counter. When she faces me, her hand grips a knife.

*Well, this has taken a turn.*

"I meant, use your words, although I approve of your commitment." I hold my palms up in surrender.

Roe's eyes flit between me and the blade, and then she smirks, like she finds the situation funny. Before I can make another comment, the witch touches the point to her thumb and presses until a red drop wells against the stainless steel.

Every cell of my being homes in on the sight, my fangs lengthening until my mouth feels oddly full.

"You can stay, and you can drink from me when you need to." The witch extends her arm, offering her precious blood to me.

As if she thinks I'm worthy.

"You give too much of yourself." My voice breaks, as I'm desperate to be strong enough to stop taking from her.

Roe shrugs. "It's my choice."

"I fed today," I point out automatically, even as my feet move me across the kitchen.

When I stand just a foot from her, I pull on the last bit of my self-control and pause.

But then Roe sets down the knife and steps forward, her uninjured hand settling on my waist as her other cups my chin. Her bleeding thumb hovers scant inches from my lips.

"Sample then. To see if you like the taste."

**5**

———

**ROE**

THE MOVE IS bold and born of pure selfishness.

*Suck me*, I plead silently. *Take from me.*

Keta looked so forlorn when she came downstairs. Dejected.

The sight tore into my stomach, gutting me. Keta is a woman made for smiling and laughter. But she's always apologizing to me, like she expects I'll yell at her or speak harsh words. All I want is for her joy to return. And for me to be the catalyst for it.

So, I'm tempting her. The vampire has fed me every day, and I want to return the favor.

I know this is a risky offer to make, considering her secret past trauma with witches. But if the spell didn't have her panicking, maybe this won't either.

*What's the worst that could happen? She leaves?*

She was going to anyway. I saw it in her face. This time, she meant it.

Now, Keta is sober and so close. I'm touching her, although

the thick robe makes it hard to enjoy the curves of her under my palm. If only she'd cross the last inch. Wrap her lips around my thumb before the blood dries.

Eyes with wide pupils rise to meet mine, sending a stronger jolt of need through my body.

*Can she hear the thundering of my pulse? Does she know why my heart beats so hard? That the rhythm is for her?*

Maybe, if the beat is powerful enough, the vampire will sway to it, like she does with her favorite music.

"Some people think sharing blood is intimate." Keta's breath caresses my thumb. "Your girlfriend might mind."

Frustration at the pointless barrier I built bubbles over, making my next words harsh. "There's no one else. Just you."

That earns me a gasp, but before I can revel in the sound, her mouth is on me.

The first tug pairs with a surprising sting. Then, the sensation bleeds into erotic ecstasy.

Keta wraps her strong fingers around my wrist, holding me in place as she laps at my wound. Every time she sucks, I experience the grip of her lips all the way down to my clit.

*Who knew there was such a direct connection?*

Keta makes small sounds of pleasure as she tongues me, and my breath comes harsher. I slide my free hand around to her lower back, drawing the vampire's body flush against mine until I can bury my nose in her curls. The smell of the healing herbs from the bath lingers, and the scent brings back the image of her soaking, naked.

The memory has me moaning, and Keta whimpers against my hand.

*Does this feel as good for her as it does for me? Or is this just the equivalent to eating a delicious meal?*

I want to be more to her than sustenance.

"Keta," I exhale her name, not sure what question will follow.

The golden vampire releases my finger, tilting her head back to meet my stare. Her eyes aren't the dreamy haziness caused by the sun. She has a sharp focus, an intensity that causes heat to pool in my lower belly.

"You taste like raspberries. And sex."

"Kiss me," I demand. The first command I've ever given her. The only request I've ever made.

Her radiant smile is second only to the sensual drag of her lips against mine.

*Finally*, a voice in the back of my brain whispers.

Then, Keta drives all thoughts from my mind as she kisses me light at first but then deeper. She fits me, and I, her, every movement and breath becoming synchronized. I half-expected her to taste like blood, but she's a heady flavor, like the first sip of a dry wine. Already, I'm drunk on her, leaning forward, trying to sink into the tease of her lips.

There's the delectable sensation of nails trailing up the back of my neck and combing against my scalp. My nerves throb like I'm working magic, but Keta is the one who's enchanting me.

When she pulls back, I follow without thinking, trying to regain the glory of our intimacy.

"You worked all day. You should rest," she speaks the words against my mouth, as we're still so close.

A response doesn't come easy to my mind, as my thoughts linger on more tempting things. Eventually though, I form an answer.

"I'll go to bed," I concede. "But not alone."

Keta's fingers flex and then twine in the strands of my hair, and I'm about to beg her to tug on them when she releases me.

*Shit. Did I do something wrong? Is she going to leave now?*

"I'll keep you company." Keta reaches to her back, peeling my hand off, only to lace our fingers together. She pulls me toward the stairs.

I need no more direction than that, following as close as I

can without tripping her. As we ascend, her plump ass is perfectly level with my stare, and I give in to the temptation to reach out and cup a cheek.

Keta gasps, whirling around. "Did you just feel me up?"

"Maybe." I shrug, barely able to suppress a grin.

She moves down a step, still coming in a few inches taller than me. "Someone is impatient."

My captivating vampire hooks a finger in the top button on my pajamas and slides it free. My collar falls open, wide enough to reveal the shadow between my breasts. Keta traces my collarbone and then slides her touch down to that cleft and then back up again. Teasing me.

The sensation is an erotic torture, but she's not the only one who can play with seduction.

After all, the only thing between my hands and her naked body is a flimsy layer of terry cloth.

My fingers fiddle with the front flap of her robe, and then I sneak under the fabric to find her soft curls.

This was supposed to be my retaliation, but the tickle against my palm has me panting.

"Okay?" I ask, applying the barest of pressure.

Keta responds by widening her legs. An invitation.

I don't even have to dive deep to find the wetness. She's damp for me, and when I push under her hood, stroking her clit, my own responds in time.

"Roe." My name is sin on her lips.

She clutches my shoulders, and I welcome the needy bite of her grip.

The bedroom is too far away.

Keta got to taste me earlier. Now, it's my turn, and I need that flavor on my tongue as soon as possible.

Supporting her with a hand on her lower back, I encourage Keta to recline on the stairs. She sinks down fast, eager eyes watching as I kneel on the step below her.

With a quick tug, her robe falls open.

Tan skin rises and falls before me, beckoning me to explore. Her nipples, the tight buds that taunted me earlier in the sunlight, call to me now. I rise over her, wrapping my lips around the peak and sucking until she whimpers. Only then do I return to the space between her legs.

Keta's core is slick with her pleasure, and I give myself permission to feast.

When I lick my tongue over her folds, her thighs quiver where they bracket my head. As I suck on her clit, her harsh breaths echo in the stairwell.

As I worship the center of her pleasure, I slide a finger inside, reveling in the way her body clenches around me.

Keta has lived in my house, talked with me late into the night, watched me consume the food she's prepared, spoiled my familiar, and filled my once-quiet life with laughter.

And even so, there has always been a chasm of unspoken thoughts between us. A space neither of us has dared to traverse.

But when Keta wrapped her lips around my finger, pulling me inside her, a bridge started to form.

Now, as she sobs my name during her release, I claim a part of her.

This vampire, who shoved her way into my life, will soon find out I have no intention of letting her leave.

6

———

**KETA**

I WAKE up to the soothing caress of fingers combing through my hair. It's a decadent sensation that I would highly recommend.

Blinking the sleep from my eyes, I have to take a moment to orient myself.

*Oh yeah, I'm in Roe's bedroom.*

I've been in this room for almost an entire day.

After she pleasured me on the stairs, we finally made it to a bed. Her bed. Then, we spent the night hours exploring each other's bodies, only taking brief breaks for food, which resulted in the kitchen table getting as thoroughly christened as the stairs.

I don't know how she lasted for so long after working through the day, but my witch didn't pass out until just before dawn, and I followed right after. Luckily, Roe has a set of thick blackout curtains in her room, so I didn't end up stumbling from the bed in another ridiculous sun-drunk escapade.

Now, I glance at her bedside table to see it's just after six p.m., which means the sun set not too long ago. The start of a vampire's day as well as a witch when she works the night shift.

That last realization has me bolting up in bed.

"Goddess! Why are you still here?"

When I sat up so abruptly, Roe collapsed back on her pillows. As I stare down at her, I briefly lose my train of thought.

She's gorgeous. Roe's hair falls in a messy brown halo around her angular face, the strands appearing softer when they aren't slicked back. Her body is slimmer than mine but still with curves and high breasts, which are a perfect handful. Unconsciously, I reach out, intent on thumbing one of those cherry nipples, when I remember myself.

"Why aren't you up?" I push because she hasn't answered my question.

The witch quirks an eyebrow. "Because this is my bed."

"No! I mean, why aren't you getting ready for work? You're going to be late! Hell, I haven't made you anything for breakfast."

On the verge of crawling out of the sheets, I find my movement stayed by her arm around my waist.

"Calm down. I took off the next few days. For the holiday," she murmurs the words against my lower back, pressing a hot kiss to the base of my spine after each sentence.

My panic subsides as my nerves tighten with excited tingles.

Then, what she said fully registers.

*The holiday.*

*Of course.*

*Tomorrow is the winter solstice.*

A pang of longing clenches my gut. "Ah," is the only word I can get out of my mouth. I consider continuing my retreat, just so I don't risk revealing the hurt with a cringing expression.

No need for my past pain to ruin what is probably a joyful time for Roe.

"Yes, ah. We can stay in bed a bit longer." Again comes the warm pressure of her lips on my exposed skin.

I want to melt into the intimate touch so badly, but dark memories threaten to cloud my mind.

"We will have to get up at some point though. My mom is expecting me," Roe continues. "What is work like for you the next couple of days?"

"Um ..." Thoughts are sluggish, crowded out by the fantasy of having a mother who looks forward to a visit.

*Uma feels that way about me. I'm not alone anymore.*

Clearing my throat, I try to speak like this is a normal, casual conversation. "My next deadline isn't until mid-January."

Another soothing kiss brushes along the sharp angle of my shoulder blade.

"Want to come to my family's solstice celebration?" Roe asks in a brief moment her mouth isn't worshipping me.

Some sharp object lodged in my chest eases, and I find myself gasping at the relief.

"You're—" I choke, worried I might start crying. "You're inviting me?"

The solid press of her forehead settles against the base of my neck. She's slowly wrapped her body around mine without me realizing, and I can smell the salt of her sweat with the underlying tart hint of raspberries.

"Is it too big of a step?" Roe mutters the question. "Having you now, I don't want to walk away."

The sentiment clutches at my heart, and I understand how she feels. Whatever this thing is between us is new and fragile. I'm afraid if I breathe too deeply, it'll shatter.

*But does she understand what she just offered me?*

I've longed to be a part of a Yule celebration every year of my life, and now, Roe has extended the opportunity with such a casual invite.

The winter solstice. A sacred holiday for witches.

Even if I wasn't so enraptured with Roe, I doubt I'd be able to turn the offer down.

"I want to go," I whisper back. "But I'm a vampire, not a witch."

Sheets rustle behind me, and I glance over my shoulder to watch as Roe rises to her knees. The bedding falls away, and again, I'm mesmerized by the sight of her.

A strong finger hooks under my chin, tilting my head until I meet her midnight eyes. "You don't need to be a witch to celebrate Yule. This is all about gathering with family and friends to honor hearth and home and new beginnings. You'll fit in fine."

*Fit in? With witches?*

The idea seems ludicrous to me, but Roe is so confident that I can't help but allow my measly defenses to crumble.

"Yes," I say. "I'll come."

Roe's lips curl, a wicked expression, and she leans down to press an openmouthed kiss on the rapid flutter of my pulse.

But even the pleasure of her affection can't fully blot out this momentous occasion.

I'm going to a winter solstice celebration for the second time in my life.

The first took place when I was less than a year old.

After that, I was never permitted to attend again.

7

———

**ROE**

MY FAMILY'S house sits at the foothill of a mountain. Not a very tall mountain, but the street ends, and if you want to go any farther, you have to go up.

I park in the gravel drive behind a shiny Tesla.

"Are you sure it's okay that I'm here?" Keta asks.

Glancing over, I find her fiddling with the seat belt, as if reluctant to take it off.

"Of course." I cover her nervous hands with one of mine. "They don't bite."

She grimaces. "But I do."

I snort and then stifle my laughter because Keta still looks like she might refuse to leave my car.

"You're not big on family gatherings?"

*Or is it that she's not big on gatherings of witches?*

I should've thought of that. This could be a certain kind of hell for her, but she agreed to come anyway, just for my sake.

I took some precautions to make sure she'd feel more

comfortable at the actual celebration, but that won't help with this initial meeting of my relatives.

One of Keta's fangs worries her bottom lip, and I want nothing more than to lean over and lick the adorably sharp point. But I keep to myself and give her room to talk.

"I've never been to a big family gathering. Uma is my only family."

If she had punched me in the gut, it might have hurt less.

*What was her life before the night she showed up in my ER?*

*Was she homeless? Abused?*

Whatever Keta went through, I know from her drunken confession that she was definitely lonely.

And I never want her to feel that way again.

"Well, here's how a Fowler gathering usually goes. It'll be my mom, my dad, and my older sister. That's the core group, but I'm betting from the number of cars here, there are a handful of cousins. Mom is going to be all over you the minute you walk in the door. She'll probably rope you into helping with some kind of craft. Dad will offer you a drink and ask you what you do for a living. He'll actually want to know about your job, so don't spare any details. My sister, Clara, is nice but nosy and enjoys bossing people around. It'll be loud, but I think you'll fit in fine."

Keta stares at me, eyes wide. "I think that's the most words you've ever spoken to me at one time."

"Did it help?" I'll keep talking for the rest of the night if it puts her at ease.

Her smile is hesitant at first but then blooms wide. "Yeah, it did."

"Good." I squeeze her hands again. "We can leave anytime you want. Just say the word."

Keta nods and slides her grip from mine to unbuckle her seat belt. We climb from the car and meet in front of the hood. Wanting to make clear that I'm not about to take her into a den of wolves and abandon her, I scoop her hand in mine, twining our fingers together.

When we reach the front door, I don't bother to knock. The house is bright and warm as we step inside, leaving behind the chill of the last day of fall. The scent of baking bread fills the air along with some hearty spices, and I can hear laughter toward the back of the house.

"We're here!" I call out. This way, we can filter some of the introductions instead of stepping into the overwhelming madness.

"Who's here?" The excited question comes a second before my mother.

People say we look alike with our height and the way our chins curve sharply and the dark brown of our hair. Only I've chopped mine short while hers sways past her lower back.

Still, in her, I can see what I might look like in thirty years, and I'm not mad about it.

"Roe's here! And who's your friend?"

Before I can make introductions, my vampire is already stepping forward, releasing my hold so she can extend a hand. "I'm Keta Latimer. I'm so sorry for intruding on your holiday."

Mom clasps Keta's hand in both of hers, and instead of shaking it, she draws the vampire close, hugging her. "Don't be silly. The winter solstice is no fun without a few fresh faces in the mix. Latimer you said? Any relation to Uma?" Without releasing her, my mom retreats toward the kitchen, dragging my guest deeper into the house.

I try not to be put out about losing my grip on the situation and on my vampire.

"Yes, actually. She's kind of been my adoptive mom these last few years."

"That's wonderful! And did she introduce you and Roe?"

"Oh, um ..." Keta glances back at me, and I catch the twinge of panic in her gaze.

And why wouldn't she be uneasy? Meeting because of a brutal attack that left her on the edge of death is not a casual conversation you share like it's small talk.

"No," I answer in Keta's stead. "How we met is a story for another time. Just focus on not scaring Keta away for now, Mom."

Luckily, the Fowler matriarch knows when to drop something. "I'll try not to be too terrifying."

We step into the kitchen, which also bleeds into the dining room, and my family passes Keta around. She shakes hands with all my relatives while answering basic questions about herself. Trust my mom to make sure any guest is fully immersed in the group.

At this moment, I couldn't be prouder to be her daughter.

From the way Keta smiles, I can guess she's no longer doubting her welcome to our gathering.

When the introductions reach my little second cousin, the innocent-looking girl waves and then leans in close, as if to share a secret. Despite her hushed tone, she's anything but subtle.

"Do you like fire?" The six-year-old pulls a book of matches out of her pocket.

"Samara!" My cousin Amethyst slams her glass of wine down on the counter and lunges for her daughter.

"I love fire!" the child shouts and sprints from the room.

"And I hate property damage," my cousin mutters, chasing after the little pyromaniac.

Mom waves a dismissive hand after them, smiling demurely. "Don't worry about Samara," she tells the room. "I cast a dampening spell on her the minute she stepped through the door. She won't be able to do more than light a candle for weeks."

Keta's astonished expression subsides when we all chuckle.

"Would you like something to drink, Keta?" my dad asks.

"Wine would be fine."

As he pours her a glass, he asks over his shoulder, "And what is it you do for a living?"

Keta accepts the drink and gives an outline of her work as a photojournalist.

"That's amazing," my mother breathes. "And you must have an artistic eye. Would you mind helping Amethyst with weaving our Yule crowns? It's important there's enough for everyone to wear tomorrow night."

Mom gestures toward the dining table. There's a pile of greenery in the middle of the surface. Sprigs of holly, strands of ivy, and small cuts of evergreen branches. Pinecones of different sizes lie scattered about. Plenty of foliage to cover everyone's heads.

"I'd love to," Keta says. There's something in her voice that catches my attention, but when I turn to look at her, she's facing away from me.

The evening continues on like the night before the winter solstice normally does. My parents bake and prep ingredients for tomorrow's holiday feast. They'll have at least four Crock-Pots cooking away with hearty stews to keep us warm and full on the longest night of the year. While they work, we're all supposed to be the entertainment, maintaining a steady stream of conversation that keeps everyone awake while also resolidi-fying the bonds of family.

We reflect on our favorite memories from the past year, and a warm glow fills my chest as I sink easily back into our family dynamic.

What surprises me is how seamlessly Keta fits in. Of course, I fully expected the Fowlers to welcome her. But it's not long before she's making everyone laugh with tales of her photog-raphy mishaps, like the night she got locked on a roof in pursuit of the perfect angle and then had to climb down the rickety fire escape, only to accidentally spy on the building's residents through their wide-open curtains.

"One lady had so many porcelain dolls in her bedroom, I was sure she was filming some sort of horror movie." Keta affects an alarmed expression that has Samara snickering. The little girl has practically climbed into Keta's lap as she watches the vampire's deft hands weave foliage into neat headdresses. "Then, a few floors down, there was a man singing karaoke."

"That doesn't sound so weird," Amethyst points out.

"It wouldn't have been. Except he was dressed head to toe in some kind of superhero getup. I'm talking full-body spandex. Luckily, he had a mask on because if I ever ran into him, I'd never be able to look in his eye. There is not an inch of his body that I don't know the shape of now. And, Goddess, I've never seen such vigorous thrusting."

The room erupts in laughter.

As the chuckles die off, Clara stands from her barstool to grab a fresh gingersnap cookie from the cooling rack. "Want one, Keta?" she asks, pointing to the remaining dozen.

"No, thank you." My vampire keeps her eyes on her glue gun.

"You haven't had anything to eat since you got here. Roe is neglecting you. We have so much dessert. Just tell me what sounds good." My sister already has the fridge open, pulling out pies.

"Clara, she's not hungry." My exasperation bleeds into my voice.

"Come on. You must have eaten hours ago, and we need to stay up all night. Hence, sugary foods. So, what'll it be, Keta? Pie? Muffins? Amethyst brought over these cranberry cream cheese tarts that are addictive."

"That's okay," Keta says, her tone almost embarrassed. "I'm … well, I … I'm a vampire."

The noise in the room dims, and I watch as Keta's body goes stiff.

*Is this what she was worried about in the car? That my family would judge her for what she is?*

I wish I had known. I could have easily allayed her fears.

"You are?" Samara screeches the question, standing on the bench seat to stare in wonder at my guest. "That's so cool! Do you drink Roe's blood?"

A memory replays in my mind of Keta's tongue caressing my finger. From the blush stealing over the vampire's cheeks, she's thinking the same thing.

"I have. Once," she mutters, staring intently at the crown she's weaving, as if it required the same amount of attention as defusing a bomb.

"That's awesome! What does she taste like?"

Children. Absolutely no boundaries.

Keta clears her throat, eyes flicking to me and then back to her hands. "Raspberries."

*And sex*, I add silently, recalling her description. But the kid doesn't need to know that.

"I wonder what I taste like," Amethyst ponders, as curious as her daughter.

"Get your own vampire," I growl at my cousin, moving to stand behind mine, resting my hands on her shoulders.

Amethyst sticks her tongue out at me, making Samara giggle.

Keta glances up at me, her smile bordering on shy. Then, so fast that I almost miss it, she presses a fleeting kiss to the back of my hand before returning to her crafting.

I fight not to grin like an idiot, but I'm sure I fail.

"Sorry for being pushy." Clara restocks the unwanted desserts, and Keta waves away her apology.

It's a while later, after the crowns sit in a finished pile, that Samara convinces Keta to put on a display of her supernatural strength. The two turn on the outside spotlights and head to the backyard. I watch through the window as the young witch cheers my vampire on in a riding-lawn-mower dead lift.

At least Samara isn't playing with her matches anymore.

Although I can't hear them through the glass, I can see the joy in Keta's laughing mouth and bright eyes.

"Goddess, you're smitten, aren't you?" Clara's voice has me turning to meet her mocking smile.

It's on the tip of my tongue to deny it. A knee-jerk reaction after decades of teasing from my sister. But I realize she's only speaking the truth.

"What gave me away?"

"Well, you stare at her like she's your favorite movie, set on replay. And then there's the fact that you invited her not only to meet all of us, but also to do it on the solstice." She hooks both thumbs in the pockets of her designer jeans. Being a hotshot lawyer in Richmond pays well. "So, is this thing serious?"

If everything was solely up to me, the answer would be easy.

*Yes.*

But relationships take two people, and Keta still holds a lot of herself back.

A deep sigh pushes out my nose. "I want it to be. But I can't help thinking I'm going to mess it up."

"Why's that?"

I shrug. "We're doing things out of order. She's basically living at my place, but that's going to end soon. How do I keep her interest when she's not sleeping down the hall?" *Or in the bed with me, like we did this past day?*

Clara scoffs, "I think you should give Keta and yourself more credit. Do you really think these feelings are all proximity-based?"

"Not for me," is all I can definitively say.

My sister stares at me, and I try not to fidget. If this inquisition can help me hold on to Keta, then I'll gladly go through it time and again.

"Okay. Let's say, Keta finishes whatever she has going on in town, and she heads out, but she's still interested in continuing things. What'll you do?"

The thought of Keta loading up in her van and leaving on the road trip she's talked about hurts my chest. But I breathe through the pain to speak my answer, "I'll figure it out. Talk on the phone. Video chat. Take a vacation to visit wherever she ends up."

With a smile, Clara reaches out to squeeze my shoulder. "That sounds like a good plan to me. Now, you just need to talk to Keta about it."

"I know," I mutter. But talking to Keta about dating long distance feels like I'd be pushing her to leave.

"Don't look so glum. This is the perfect time for this to happen. Use the magic of Yule to lend power to your bond. This is when you want to forge new connections. To plan for the new year."

Clara is right. Magic is a subtle pulse in the air. A pressure that will only build until it reaches its pinnacle tomorrow night.

But to take advantage of the power, to build something lasting, I'll need Keta to be on board with me.

Which means I need her to trust me.

To share some of her secrets.

8

———

**ROE**

"Get a good day's rest! The real celebration starts tomorrow night." As Mom ushers Keta and me toward the stairs, I shoulder the duffel bag we packed before coming over.

"Are we sharing a room?" Keta asks when we reach the upstairs landing. At my nod, she offers a ridiculous leer. "Scandalous."

I don't bother suppressing a snort, and I grab her hand to turn into the second door on the left. My childhood bedroom.

Keta seems to realize this the moment we step over the threshold because she immediately begins to snoop.

"You played volleyball?" Her fingers trail over the display of trophies neatly arranged on the shelf.

"In high school."

She squints at the picture of our championship team. "Do you still have the tight little shorts?"

"Hmm. Why would you want to know about those?"

She shrugs. "No reason," she says, her tone full of feigned nonchalance.

59

Despite her seductive jokes, Keta keeps wandering around, asking questions about some of the items she finds. Discovering more and more about my past.

And I still know nothing of hers.

My conversation with Clara plays in my head again, and I suddenly feel like the solstice magic exists in an hourglass, the small grains of sand slipping away so fast that I'll lose my chance to take advantage of them.

To keep Keta with me for more than just this temporary visit.

I need to know more of her, or we might lose this fragile connection as the previous year fades into the new one.

"Tell me something I don't know," I blurt without thinking.

Keta sets down the plush rainbow owl my dad gave me the day after I came out to my parents and turns to look at me. "The first photograph of a human was taken in 1838. The guy was getting his shoes shined."

Her random fact eases some of the tension in my chest.

"I meant, something I don't know about *you*."

The vampire stares at me for a stretch of time that is probably only a few seconds but drags on like days.

"I'm assuming you want to hear something more than just what my favorite color is?"

"I want to know you," I press.

She nods, and I watch as one extra-sharp canine sneaks out to worry her lower lip. The sight has my nipples hardening, but I ignore the reaction. Sex can come later—after I get a peek behind the curtain.

With a soul-deep sigh, Keta gives me what I asked for.

"I hated you."

Turns out, I should be careful what I wish for. "You hated me?"

"For an entire year, the thought of you filled me with a terrible, burning rage." Keta fists a hand over her heart, like that's where the hatred lived.

The idea that the woman I'm falling for ever hated me makes my breath come faster.

*Do those feelings still linger somewhere in the back of her mind?*

"Why?" I whisper.

Keta's hand unclenches, and she offers me a small, sad smile. "Because you saved my life."

The explanation settles between us, and I try to decipher what she could mean. "And that made you hate me?"

The vampire abandons my dresser and moves to the window, unlocking the latch so she can push it open. Old wood creaks in protest but is no match for her strength. A chill fills the room, the air having dropped to almost freezing once the sun set. Keta sucks in a deep lungful, as if she's been holding her breath for a while now.

"I went to the nest on purpose," she finally says.

The word doesn't register at first, but then my knowledge of the supernatural world provides a definition.

*The nest.* A term vampires use when they live together in groups. Like the gathering that must've dealt a younger Keta the collection of injuries I fought so hard to save her from.

*She went there on purpose?*

"Why?" I have to clear my throat of panic. "Why would you do that?"

"I wanted to die." Keta makes the admission as she faces the window, speaking to the night instead of me. "I'd wanted to die for a while at that point. But I could never go through with it. Something always stopped me. Then, I was dancing at some shitty nightclub, and I saw this guy." She waves her hand in the space left by the open window, as if the man were standing just outside my parents' house. "He should've blended in fine, but there was an oddness to his movements, like they were a second too fast. And I knew he was supernatural. He was focused on this girl. She looked so young. I would've put money down that she'd used a fake ID to get into the club. So, when he wrapped his arm around her and they left, I followed."

*Of course she did.* Whatever life Keta lived before she knew me, I could never see her abandoning a young woman to a potentially dangerous fate.

"I found them a few streets down. He pulled her into an alley, had his eyes on hers, and he was telling her things. Listing off commands."

"A Midnighter?" I ask.

Keta nods.

Different strains of vampires have unique powers. While Keta can walk in the sun and challenge a giant to an arm-wrestling match, Daylighters have no persuasive abilities. Meanwhile, Midnighters can dive into weaker minds, making the person their living puppet.

"From what he was telling her, I knew she wouldn't survive the night. The plans he laid out, they were as lethal as a loaded gun." Keta turns to me then, her expression pleading. "I know it won't make sense to you, but I wasn't scared. Not for me. There was no way I could fight him off. There was only offering him something easier."

"What did you do?" It takes all the effort I can muster to affect a steady tone. This woman I'm gone for is detailing the steps toward her almost death.

"I used the back of my earring to cut my wrist. Not to bleed out. More to grab his attention. Then, I just walked up to him and asked that he take me instead." She shrugs. "The minute he scented my blood, the girl was invisible. He took me back to his nest. Three others were waiting."

Keta still won't look at me, but that's probably better. I need a moment to smooth away whatever horrified expression is on my face.

"Anyway, I'm sure you can guess what happened next. You saw the aftermath."

I did. Her pale, bruised face paints itself across my memory, the image more gut-wrenching with every recall, because every minute, I fall more in love with this woman. The knowledge of her past pain tears at me.

"How did you get away?"

"Get away?" Keta appears confused, shaking her head. "They drank their fill and then dumped my body. I think they were leaving that night, and I was just a pre-trip snack."

*Goddess, she talks about herself like she's a bag of chips.*

"I remember smelling garbage. And watching a set of legs walk away. Then, it all went black, and I woke up in the hospital with Uma's wrist against my mouth, drinking her blood."

Now more than ever, I'm thankful my old tutor picked up her phone and was able to make the normally six-hour drive in almost half the time. If Uma hadn't given Keta a proper dose of vampire blood, the woman would have died when my powers ran out of juice.

I was so close to losing her, and even though Keta is here, more durable than ever, I can't fully eradicate the panic.

"You're"—I suck in a deep breath to keep from gasping —"not still thinking that way. Are you?"

"No!" Her adamant denial helps ease the heavy weight on my chest.

Keta abandons the window to come stand in front of me. She gathers my hands in hers, clutching them to her chest. "The people who raised me didn't love me. For the longest time, I felt alone. Abandoned and hopeless. That's why I did what I did." Keta's mouth forms into a tentative smile. "But Uma showed me love. And I discovered a job I am passionate about. It took some time, but I finally realized what you did for me wasn't a curse. It was a gift. A second chance. I am so happy to be alive." The vampire leans forward, pressing a gentle kiss against first my left and then my right cheekbone.

And a conviction settles deep in my soul.

*Uma isn't the only one who is going to show Keta what love is.*

Pulling her against me, I savor the sensation of all her soft curves molding into my body.

"I'm happy you're alive too," I murmur against her curls. The words are inadequate. I'm not merely happy. I'm desperately joyful while simultaneously terrified that her life was ever on the knife's edge of ending.

The sudden urge to care for her in any way I can comes on a wave of desperation. I need to make her as strong as possible, so death will never be foolish enough to try taking her from me.

"Are you hungry?" Any vein my vampire wants, she can have.

"I don't need to feed very often." Keta slowly rubs her hands up and down my back, as if she knows I'm in need of soothing. "I could go another few weeks and be fine."

"What would happen if you bit me now?"

Her caress pauses and then slides lower to finger the waistband of my jeans. "I wouldn't take much. And getting a taste of you would have me wanting to do other things."

Leaning back so I can meet her eyes, I tilt my head to the side in invitation.

The second Keta's fangs pierce my skin, lust infuses every cell of my being. It's not long before we're on the bed, stripping each other of clothes. She barely allows me one touch of her core before my vampire slides down my body to worship my clit.

An hour later, after we've both come a handful of times, I get up to close the window. Shivers skitter through my body as the frosty air meets the sweat on my skin. Once the glass sits shut, I make sure the curtains fully block out the sunlight cresting over the treetops. Crawling back into bed, I gather Keta close, pushing my fingers through her hair so I can massage her scalp.

She yawns widely before snuggling into me.

"You should stay in Roanoke." The longing words are out of my mouth before I consider how selfish they are.

"Of course I'm staying," Keta murmurs against my collarbone, momentarily giving me euphoria. But she takes it away just as fast. "I haven't finished what I came to do."

The last word is barely audible, and the next second, my vampire's breathing has evened out into sleep.

And I'm left awake, holding on to the woman I love as I fear the future.

## 9

**KETA**

"Everyone, in the cars!" Mrs. Fowler announces to the house, waving our collection of people toward the front door.

"Where are we going?" I ask. Each tradition is an amazing new discovery, and the fact that Roe's family shares them so freely warms me to my toes.

"We gather with others of our kind and light a bonfire. A light to guide us through the longest night of the year." Mrs. Fowler squeezes my shoulder, and then she grabs a set of keys and exits the house.

Roe jogs down the steps with Clara not far behind.

"Are you sure it's okay I come? Since I'm not a witch?" The fabric of my coat wrinkles in my twisting grasp as I consider hanging it back up.

Before Roe can answer, her sister does, "Neither am I."

The admission has the ground under me shifting. "You … you're not?"

The eldest Fowler grins. "Nope. Born to a family of witches but not a drop of magic in me." She wraps a scarf around her neck. "I was salty about it for a few years, but now, I'm glad that if it had to be one of us, it was me."

"Seriously?" Roe is apparently learning this info the same time I am.

Clara nods. "You're the one interested in healing people. What would I have done with it? Fixed all the paper cuts I got from flipping through court briefings?" She pauses, looking thoughtful, and then gives Roe a mock glare. "I changed my mind. I want it. Give it!" Her hands make grabby motions.

Roe snorts. "Sorry, sis. No takebacks."

Their banter is one of my favorite things to watch. The easy affection that this entire family has hurts my heart because it's so beautiful.

What rocks me to my core is the knowledge that Clara isn't a witch, but her family doesn't treat her any differently than Roe or Amethyst or Samara.

When Roe's eyes meet mine, I can tell by her raised brows that my confused shock must be clear on my face. My initial impulse is to smooth them away, covering my inner turmoil with a cheery smile.

But I don't.

Instead, I let Roe see that something about this exchange has affected me.

"Keta?"

Stepping in close, I wrap my arms around her neck and press my lips against her ear. "I promise to tell you later." When I lean back, I offer a gentle, honest smile. "Right now, I cannot wait to see this bonfire."

"You're not the only one." Clara rolls her eyes as she reaches to open the door. "Everyone has to be on Samara duty tonight. I wouldn't put it past the kid to try climbing into the thing. You'd think she was a fire elemental with her obsession."

Roe and I follow her out and get in a car with Mrs. and Mr. Fowler. The drive only takes ten minutes, but for that short time, I'm suddenly a teenager again. Or maybe for the first time since I didn't exactly have a normal childhood. As Roe and I sit in the backseat, our hands cross the short distance between us, clasping and then fiddling with fingers, the tiny yet suggestive strokes a silent conversation.

By the time we reach our destination, my face is burning, my cheeks full of Roe's blood, no doubt.

Our group pulls into the driveway of a cute house. The cottage sits, surrounded by trees on all sides. A dark-haired woman stands on the front porch, waving to us. She comes out to greet everyone as we pile out of the cars. Roe introduces me, and I shake hands with Virginia Henwood, this year's winter solstice host.

"We cleared a nice space out back. We were waiting for more people to show up to light everything," the woman explains as she leads us around to the rear of her house.

There, we find another woman holding a flashlight and a man stacking thick logs of wood. He seems to arrange them in a certain formation, under the direction of his companion.

A dog lies, sprawled out in the grass beside them. At our approach, the animal lifts a blockish head, lets out a disinterested huff, and then falls immediately back asleep.

Someone seems to disapprove of the late hour.

"Can I light it? Please!" The begging comes from behind me, and I glance back to see Samara tugging on her mother's hand.

Amethyst sighs. "I shouldn't let you, little menace. But tradition does call for a child to bring on the light of the new year."

Samara cheers, and I chuckle. Yet another element of this Yule celebration I can add to my happiness hoard. A long time ago, I was told I'd receive these tidbits of knowledge. I was promised the secrets of all the witches' celebrations, but that vow was soon revoked when I was deemed unworthy. Eventually I gave up hope of ever learning.

The urge to document each second of this night overwhelms me.

From my bag, I pull out my camera. Well, one of them anyway. This model is a portable size.

"Do you think it would be okay if I took some pictures? I want to remember this night," I throw the question out to the group, giving everyone an opportunity to object.

No one does. The exact opposite.

"Of course you can," Mrs. Henwood exclaims as Roe offers me an encouraging smile. "And I would love it if you shared them. I always forget, but it's important to have mementos. If only to help our memories years down the line."

"That's exactly my thinking," I say, knowing an answering grin sits on my face.

Our party gathers near the firepit, and Mrs. Fowler hands around the crowns I weaved last night. Maybe it's silly, but when no one complains about wearing my foliage creations, pride fills my chest to the brim. Not only am I attending, but I'm also *helping* with the Yule celebration.

Mrs. Fowler winks as she hands me the headpiece I specifically requested, and Roe smirks when I settle the masterpiece on my temple.

The entire circlet is formed from mistletoe.

"What?" I ask my witch. "Too obvious?"

She snorts but then drops a lingering, sweet-as-berries kiss on my lips. Clearly, I made the perfect Yule crown.

"Are we waiting for the others to arrive?" Mr. Fowler asks as he drops an armload of logs at the edge of the pit.

"We don't have to. They'll get here when they get here, and it's too cold to linger without some heat." Ms. Henwood waves Roe's little cousin forward.

Amethyst hands her daughter a match, which Samara expertly lights. Despite her enthusiasm, the girl is careful as she squats down to put the flame to the tiny pile of flammable twigs. Once those catch, she tosses the match into the growing blaze and moves back to her mother's side.

For a few minutes, we all stand quietly, watching as the beginning of a fire struggles to stay alive, sparks searching for fuel to consume. Soon enough, larger branches catch, and the hungry flames move on to the logs. It's not long before we have a proper-sized bonfire going.

People break off their mesmerized gazing and strike up conversations. Old friends and family catching up.

Night photo shoots are my specialty, obviously. I've gotten adept at finding light when there's not much around. Tonight though, the light source is obvious.

Every shot I take, firelight illuminates the focus of the picture. The effect is gorgeous, blending a reddish glow with a shadowy darkness.

I'm just capturing Roe laying another log on the flames when her mother sidles up to me.

"Here." Mrs. Fowler holds out her hand. "Go stand by her. I can't promise my skills are anywhere near yours, but it'd be nice to have one of you two together, wouldn't it?"

"Yes, definitely." I pull the neck strap over my head and carefully hand off my camera before going to stand by Roe.

"I don't remember volunteering to model," my witch mutters, even as humor curls her lips.

The blaze of the flames reflects in her dark irises. I could stare, enraptured, until the fire burns out.

But I push that urge to the side.

"Shut up and pretend you like me," I demand, wrapping my arms around her waist, practically plastering myself to her side. There's a desperation in my hold. A longing to claim this night and this life I'm imagining, where I can have a woman, a family, who cares for me.

Hopefully, my smile doesn't appear manic in the picture.

Just as the click of the shutter sounds, Roe's lips press

against the side of my head. "This is the best Yule I've ever had," she whispers in my ear as Mrs. Fowler snaps a few more shots of us.

No doubt, I look like a dumbfounded, lovesick idiot in every one.

A sharp bark breaks through my haze of infatuation and draws my attention to the dog I spotted on our arrival. No longer napping, the creature is on all fours, the muscular body wiggling in excitement.

Noir lets out a disgruntled caw from above, where she's settled on a fat branch. The bird has me drawing a conclusion.

"Pit bull familiar?" I ask Roe, wondering who found their magical partner in the spirit of a canine.

When my witch doesn't immediately answer, I meet her eyes. Sparks from the bonfire continue to reflect in her dark gaze, and she grins at me, as if I'm missing something.

"What?"

Still no answer, just a tilt of her head so I can peer over her shoulder.

And that's when I see the new arrival. Someone I know.

"Uma!" Letting go of Roe, I sprint across the clearing.

My vampire sire walks out from the line of trees with a maternal smile on her face.

I fully intend to wrap the woman in my arms, but a mangy beast blocks my way. That's when I realize why the other dog was barking.

"You got a dog?"

When I left Ohio, the only animals Uma had in her life were a few stray cats she left food out for and a handful of raccoons that sometimes beat the cats to the bowls. But there's rope tied around the pup's neck, the other end of the tether resting in Uma's hand.

The scruffy dog attempts to place both front paws on my

shoulders, and I have to hold back my strength so as not to hurt the creature when I shove it off.

"Oh, honey. It's so good to see you." Uma maneuvers around the slobbering animal to wrap me in a one-armed hug. In her embrace, everything seems right in the world.

I'm not sure if winter solstice magic works on vampires. Everything I was told, growing up, maintained that this power was reserved for witches. But some force envelops me along with Uma's loving gesture, leaving me balanced and invigorated. Like my soul just went through the washing machine, and now, I'm free of the dirt and residue from the past year.

"Good to see you too. But seriously, a dog?"

She laughs, stepping back. "He's not mine. I found him wandering just down the road. I thought he might belong to someone here. Or that they might know where his home is."

No one mentioned misplacing a dog, but Virginia might know if her neighbors are looking.

Before I can say as much, a screech fills the night air. "Fireball!"

Samara sprints toward us, her stare locked on the dog, her arms outstretched. The animal yaps a joyful sound and vigorously wags his tail when the girl bear-hugs him.

"Oh good." Uma's relief is a sigh in her voice. "This is your puppy?"

"Yes," Samara says.

"No," Amethyst responds at the same time as her daughter, joining our group with a few more from the party following behind. "We do not have a dog."

"We didn't have a dog," Samara comes right back with. "Now, we do. We have Fireball." Then, a strangely definitive quality enters the young witch's voice. "He's mine."

Everyone around us stiffens, and then as a group, they bow their heads. The display only has a second to be creepy because the next moment, the entire gathering is cheering.

"What is happening?" I mutter to Roe as she approaches my side.

Her grin is infectious, although I'm still not sure why everyone is celebrating.

"Samara found her familiar. Or it seems, her familiar found her." Roe settles a hand on my lower back. "Doesn't happen every day."

"Fine," Amethyst mutters, holding her hand out for the leash. "I guess we have a dog."

Even though the woman sounds aggrieved, I'm certain I spot a slight upward curve to the corner of her mouth.

"Didn't know you would be so helpful when I invited you." Roe steps forward to offer Uma a hug.

Now that the vampire has two free arms, she's able to fully embrace my ...

*My what exactly?*

Roe and I hooked up a few times. She invited me to a sacred holiday with all of her family. I revealed a dark piece of my past to her.

*So, she's my girlfriend? My partner? My late-night lover?*

Once the hellos are over, I think it's time to find out.

As Roe and Uma catch up, Mrs. Fowler sidles up to me, handing over my camera.

"I'm going to want a copy of these."

A glow shines from her eyes, the set just as dark and mysterious as her daughter's. And I'm suddenly certain that I have at least one ally on the *make Roe commit to me* front.

"Thank you." Hopefully, she can pick up the sincerity in my response. The devotion I have to ensuring her daughter's happiness.

When I navigate to the most recent shots on the little digital screen, the borrowed blood in my veins heats with happy longing. The witch stands tall and steady, gazing down at me with a half-smile pulling at her sinful lips.

I, meanwhile, appear ready to climb her.

The picture shows just how gone I am for Roe Fowler.

*Maybe I should stay behind the lense from now on.*

"You two are adorable together," Roe's mom whispers as she tilts her head to see the image.

Briefly, I wonder if I've ever felt so content as I do in this moment.

So, of course, the universe decides to puncture that bliss like an overfilled balloon.

"Mariketa?"

My spine goes rigid at both the name and the familiar voice speaking it.

*No. Please. Not right now.*

Sensing my distress, Roe eases off her conversation with Uma, glancing between me and the speaker. Uma's gaze follows, and all her happiness morphs into fury.

My sire finally shows a glimpse of the power and menace our kind can wield.

Not much in this world can demolish her caring nature. But I know one thing that does.

Slowly, I turn, praying to every goddess that I won't have to deal with this tonight. That I can enjoy this celebration and not think about why this is the first time I'm getting to do so.

Unfortunately, when my eyes alight on the person who said my name, I know my praying was too late.

"Mother."

## 10

————

**KETA**

"Wʜᴀᴛ ᴀʀᴇ ʏᴏᴜ ᴅᴏɪɴɢ ʜᴇʀᴇ?"

That's the first thing my mother says after not seeing me since I was eighteen years old.

Not, *How are you?*

Not, *Thank the gods you're alive!*

Not even, *Where have you been?*

All she wants to know is why I'm encroaching upon her sacred place.

Meeting her eyes, I blink in surprise at how different she looks. Not that she's changed much since I was a teenager. Only she doesn't have the same towering, intimidating presence that cowed me for my entire childhood.

And it's that shift that keeps me from shrinking under her glare and mumbling apologies, hoping to avoid her anger.

I'm not the shamed little girl anymore.

"I was invited." Tilting my chin toward Roe, I realize Mrs. Fowler has moved closer to me, and Virginia Henwood has left off congratulating Samara to join our side group.

75

Then, Uma comes to stand behind me, placing two solidifying hands on my shoulders. My sire might want to lay into my mother, but she also knows this fight is mine.

From the way the skin whitens around my mother's lips, I can tell she's grinding her teeth. I guess she's interested in keeping some kind of good face for these other witches. No previous time in my life has she curbed herself from chewing me out.

"I'm lost." Roe's eyes flit between me and the woman who gave birth to me. "Nell Barnes is your mother?"

Apparently, all the witches of Roanoke know each other. If my family had ever included me in this part of their life, I might have been aware of that fact.

"Mariketa Barnes?" Virginia whispers the name, connecting the dots.

My nod is jerky but not hesitant. I want Roe to know the truth about me. That way, there's nothing between us. "My birth name. But I changed it after turning. Besides"—I finger my camera with a rueful smile—"Latimer sounds more badass. More in line with a nighttime photojournalist."

My mother's stare locks on my camera, and her hands clench into fists. At this point, I doubt there's an inch of her body that is relaxed.

"Are you photographing this?" The horror in her voice makes clear what she thinks about the possibility.

Roe's mom picks up on the sentiment as well. "Calm down, Nell. It's a solstice celebration. The things we do here are sacred but not exactly secret. It's not as if Keta is distributing copies of our grimoires to the public."

"And can we get back to the important thing at hand here?" Virginia Henwood stands tall, glaring at my mother. "Because I'm not about to forget the fact that you told us your daughter *died.*"

Uma's grip tightens, and Roe stiffens beside me, sliding her hand into mine to pull me closer.

To the deepest part of my being, I appreciate the silent comfort. Because *ouch*. That my mother claimed I was dead isn't a shock, but that doesn't make it sting any less.

"She did die," Nell Barnes insists. "Did you all forget how vampires are created? Or do you not know what she is?"

"Of course we know what Keta is." Mrs. Fowler's voice is light with bafflement. "What I don't understand is why I've never met her before. How has Keta never attended one of our gatherings in all these years?"

"I don't appreciate being interrogated." My mother glowers at the group.

Her defensiveness only brings on a suffocating wave of exhaustion.

*Why does she have so much hate in her?* She's never allowed me close enough to even come up with a theory.

Worried that this situation will devolve into a shouting match, I decide to lay out the facts. "I'm not a witch. I never showed any signs of magic. That's why I was never brought to the meetings or celebrations or whatever else you all do. I was never taught anything about witchcraft. When I turned eighteen, they asked me to leave." *Told* is more like it. "We haven't had any contact since then."

Silence descends over our little gathering. Roe's fingers encircle mine, almost painfully tight, and she stares into the darkened trees, blinking rapidly. Following the direction of her gaze, I spot Noir perched on a branch. I wonder if the familiar is providing the witch any kind of comfort. I know Roe cares about me, and discovering the darkness of my past must not be fun to hear.

Mrs. Fowler and Ms. Henwood don't give up their indignation. The pair direct matching looks of fury toward Nell.

"Kicking her out was our last hope of raising her powers," my mother says, her tone defensive.

The scoff behind me lets everyone know just how ridiculous Uma believes that to be.

But the reasoning isn't unfounded.

If someone is a witch, there are three times in their lives when powers could reveal themselves. The first is almost immediately within a year of birth. The second is during puberty. When a witch's body changes, it's like an earthquake cracks a previously hidden cavern open and the power spills out.

The third time is during a great trauma.

The problem is, my parents' plan was flawed. Being kicked out wasn't a great trauma. Feeling abandoned by my family was a daily occurrence.

Being mauled by vampires, on the other hand, *that* I had known would be the final trial. The one that would release the magic or kill me.

But the terrifying event did neither, and I am finally content with the outcome.

"This is unforgivable," Mrs. Fowler whispers harshly, just as my father appears at my mother's shoulder.

For a moment, he merely seems confused by the tense group, and then his eyes alight on me and widen as if I were the ghost of his abandoned child.

*Oh wait, I am.*

"She was an adult!" My mother continues to defend her past choices. "Plenty of children leave the house at that age."

"What about the eighteen years before that? Keeping her from the coven was a different sort of cruelty. She doesn't need magic to be one of us," Mrs. Fowler hisses.

"Yes, she does! These traditions are for witches alone."

"Get your head out of your ass, Nell." Roe's mom is full-on growling now.

*Is this what mama-bear anger looks like?*

I bet if I turned around, Uma would have a similar ferocity twisting her face.

"We're not living during the inquisition. Keta should have been coming to our gatherings her whole life. And if you won't treat her as the beloved daughter you should, then we will." Then, shocking me, Mrs. Fowler lays her hand on my shoulder beside Uma's. The gesture demands nothing from me. She simply holds on to me in silent support.

And with that move, I find I can finally say what I've needed to for years. What I came to this town a month ago to do.

"I forgive you."

My parents rear back, as if I slapped them simultaneously.

Before they can spew something nasty at me, I carry on, "I'm not sure why you couldn't love me as I was. Honestly, I'm not sure love is something you all are capable of, which is sad. But now, I know it's not my fault. Still, I forgive you."

Just as my mother opens her mouth, a scowl on her face, I hold up a hand to stop her. Maybe it's the shock of my gesture that keeps her words at bay because the goddess knows she's never taken direction from me before.

"Forgiveness is something I can give, no matter if you want it or not. I don't care what you do with it. The point is that I'm done with that part of my life. I'm moving on from it and from you. I have a new mother who loves me unconditionally." Glancing behind me, I meet Uma's eyes, only to see a glimmer of tears in them. Thank the goddess she's here, my true mother, lending me her strength and support in this last confrontation. But she's not the only one I'm able to lean on. "And I have the Fowlers."

For a moment, I'm worried I've claimed something that isn't truly mine. But then Roe brings our clasped hands to her mouth, pressing a reassuring kiss to my knuckles.

"You have the Henwoods too." Virginia bows her head to

me, and I realize her daughter and son-in-law are standing not far away, each offering a nod of agreement.

"You also have the Cartwells." A melodic voice floats from the darkness between trees. A moment later, a group of five steps into the light cast by the bonfire. The leader is a mature woman with black hair curling around a set of wise eyes. The four behind her are younger with similar features, leading me to believe another of Roanoke's witch families has joined us. "We heard enough to know which side we're on. The vampire is welcome."

Nell Barnes's teeth are likely to crack if she grinds them any harder.

"This isn't the way things are done." My father finally adds his voice to the mix. He normally lets my mother lead the conversation, but it seems he's picked up on the fact that she's seconds away from screeching.

And he wouldn't want me taking his silence as dissent from her, of course.

"Our coven has never agreed to bar non-magic users from holiday gatherings," the new arrival says. "And the fact that you did so to your own daughter—not to mention, spreading lies about her death—shows your disinterest in family, one of the connections most important to embrace during Yule." The Cartwell woman moves closer, eventually coming to stand in between my parents and me. "If anyone is tainting the holiness of this gathering, it is you both."

Despite the ground staying steady under my feet, the world around me seems to rotate. Or maybe it's my view of the world that's shifting.

All my life, I thought witches would dislike, even despise, me. First, for the sin of being born without magic and then for living as a vampire.

But here I am, at a gathering of their kind, surrounded by

their support. Witches are defending my right to exist how and where I want, and they're standing against my parents to do it.

A pressure behind my eyes warns of tears, but I swallow them back, not wanting to ruin this amazing occurrence by turning into a sobbing mess.

"I want you off my property." Virginia glares at the two Barnes witches. "And when Yule has passed, I will call a convening of the coven to discuss your transgressions."

"Maybe it's best if you start seeking a new coven to align with," Roe's mom adds.

*Holy goddess. Are they kicking my parents out?*

From the disbelief and even tinge of fear in the Barnes' eyes, my guess is yes.

The group of Cartwell witches silently surrounds the two who gave me my first life. Without a word, the strangers use the force of their wills to escort my parents back toward Virginia's house and away from my newfound family.

Neither my mother nor my father tries to apologize to me. They don't even look back.

And again, their actions hurt like a throbbing hornet sting on my heart.

But I know I'll heal with time. Especially because I'm not on my own anymore.

When I turn to face Roe, I find her wearing an expression I've never seen before.

Something dark and dangerous.

Noir caws on a branch over our heads, the bird's voice an ominous warning that pairs well with the deadly promise in Roe's eyes.

My witch looks downright lethal.

When she speaks, her tone is shockingly conversational, the steady cadence of her voice an odd pair with her words.

"I think I might murder your parents."

# 11

**ROE**

Keta laughs, as if she thinks I'm joking.

But I could do it. I could stop the blood from circulating in their veins. I could halt the breath in their lungs or short-circuit the electrical pulses that keep their brains operating.

Witches refer to my magic as *healing*, but truly, they should call it *control*. I can control a body's ability to function. I've only exerted my power to improve those functions.

With the Barnes, I'm tempted to shut it all down.

No wonder Uma warned me about Keta and her past with witches. She dealt with two witches who told her she was less than nothing because she wasn't like them. Her own parents.

I'm surprised my vampire was willing to be around me for five minutes, much less stay in my house for a month.

Something in my face has Keta's humor fading, and she reaches up to cup my cheeks. Her hands are warm. Alive.

Goddess, she was so close to death that first night I saw her. White as a ghost and on the verge of becoming one. The memory only fuels my anger toward her parents.

"They're not worth it," she murmurs.

"They're why you tried to kill yourself," I growl back. "Seems worth it to me."

Soft lips press against mine, teasing back and forth until I relax into her kiss. As if taking that as my surrender, she tilts her chin back to smile up at me.

"I'm going to do it," I mutter, and her mouth flattens in response.

"No, you're not." Keta tangles her fingers with mine, drawing me away from everyone, just past the tree line, finding us privacy in the shadows. "You're going to let it go."

"They should be punished," I insist.

"I think getting kicked out of the coven is good enough. Besides, if I'd never walked into that vampire nest, I never would've met you." Her hopeful tone leaches away my rage against my will.

"You deserved better." My last argument. "You deserve to be loved."

*And I want to be the one to do it.*

"You think so?" Keta leans back against a tree trunk, even as her fingers reach out to fiddle with the zipper on my jacket.

"I love you." The words come as easy as breathing.

My vampire freezes, her stare locked just south of my chin.

"If you stay or if you go, either way, you'll have my love. But for the record, I want you to stay."

*Stay in my house. Stay in my bed. Stay in my life.*

"I don't want pity," she murmurs.

A scoff leaves my throat before I can stop it.

Keta glares at me, but I can't help the rueful grin I give her back.

"If anyone deserves pity, it should be me. Pity me for having to live with the sweetest, most vibrant, creative, gorgeous woman and not being able to touch her for weeks. Goddess, there were times I thought you were trying to kill me from needing you."

That little fang of hers shows itself, biting into her lower lip. A groan rattles out from deep in my chest as I step forward, dropping my forehead to rest on hers.

"I might have been trying to seduce you, just a tiny bit," Keta admits.

When I chuckle, she joins me.

Then, we stand quietly, bodies close together, the sounds of the woods surrounding us. A chill wind rattles the branches, and the sharp notes of bats squeaking sound overhead. I've never been more comfortable with the silence.

"I love you too."

Never mind. Her voice is so much better.

"You do?" I rasp out the question, praying to every goddess that I didn't conjure the words up solely from my longing.

"Yes." Keta cups the back of my head, holding my face close.

As if I had any urge to pull away.

"I've wanted you since I first saw you," she says. "But this is more than lust. You make me feel like I'm cared for. You opened your home to me, and now, it feels like mine. I want to claim you and this life I've felt teased with since coming back to town. I don't want to leave. I want to stay, to build something. I want to tie myself to you." Her grip tightens, as if she were on the verge of making those knots right now, using the short strands on my scalp.

"That's all I want." My body is light and yet grounded here with her. "You're all I want." Relief lifts an anxious weight from my chest, and I breathe in deep, the scent of pine and bonfire becoming the fragrance of the happiest night of my life. "I got you a gift."

"You did?" Keta blinks up at me until her gaze falls to my hand. The one I just dug into my back pocket.

The item is simple, but I hope she knows how much love is in it.

"A key?"

As I nod, my nose brushes against her mistletoe crown. "To my house. To *our* house."

I snuck out in the middle of the day while she was asleep and drove to the closest hardware store to get a copy made. Up until now, Keta has just plugged in the code to open my garage door to come and go. But this key, a bright yellow number that reminds me of that coat she was wearing the day she returned to my life, is solid evidence that she lives in the same space I do.

As I watch Keta's face, her expression morphs from shock to blinding joy. "You know, I've always wanted to be a witch." An eager hand snatches the key from me, and she tucks it into her pocket. "Now, I just want to be *with* one."

"But not just any witch, right?"

The vampire traces my chin with her thumb and then tilts my head to the side to give my neck a playful bite. She doesn't break the skin.

This time.

But soon, she will again. Keta will take parts of me inside her. The blood will pair well with my heart, which she has full possession of.

Heat that has nothing to do with the bonfire flushes under my skin.

"No, not just any," Keta murmurs. "I want *my* witch."

As the aroma of evergreen and burning wood surrounds us, my vampire pulls me in for a proper kiss. In the distance, Noir caws a response to a hooting owl while voices from my family and the coven rise and fall.

Keta and I linger in the shield of the forest, exchanging caresses that speak of eagerness for our future together.

A small sliver of my attention notes the comforting embrace

of magic enfolding the two of us. The silent but strong blessing of our union.

And as the fire provides a guiding light through the longest night, we follow our love into the new year.

# ACKNOWLEDGMENTS

Thank you Kate, for walking me through the intricacies of an ER visit. You are an amazing nurse!

Thank you to my beta readers Sylwia, Summer, and Katherine. You helped me find flaws, while still giving me the confidence to move forward with this story.

Thank you Jovana, as always, for your fantastic editing skills.

# ABOUT THE AUTHOR

Lauren Connolly is a Colorado Book Awards Finalist and an author of contemporary and paranormal romance stories. As a librarian, she knows the importance of citing sources, often falling down research rabbit holes when working on her novels. Lauren can never seem to stay in one place for too long, but trust that wherever she's living there is a dog who thinks he's a troll, twin cats hiding in the couch, and bookshelves bursting with the diverse stories written by the authors she loves.

# ALSO BY LAUREN CONNOLLY

Paranormal

Remembering a Witch (Seasonal Magic, Book 1)

Contemporary

You Only Need One

Rescue Me (Forget the Past, Book 1)

Only One Bed Anthology, Vol. 1

www.ingramcontent.com/pod-product-compliance
Lightning Source LLC
Chambersburg PA
CBHW032050180726
48284CB00004B/1263